the junky's christmas

and other stories

the junky's christmas

and other stories

edited by Elisa Segrave

Library of Congress Catalog Card Number: 94-66577

A catalogue record for this book is available from the
British Library on request

These stories are works of fiction. Any resemblance to persons
living or dead is purely coincidental

The right of the individual contributors to be acknowledged
as authors of their work has been asserted by them in accordance
with the Copyright, Designs and Patents Act 1988

'The Junky's Christmas' by William Burroughs first
appeared in 1989 in *Interzone* published by Viking, New York.
It is reprinted by permission of Viking, New York.

'Another Christmas' by William Trevor is taken
from *William Trevor. The Collected Stories.* published by
Viking in 1992. It is reprinted by permission of the
Peters Fraser & Dunlop Group Ltd.

The excerpt on page 120 from the Queen's Christmas message
in 1979 is quoted by kind permission of HM The Queen

First published in 1994 by
Serpent's Tail, 4 Blackstock Mews, London N4
and 401 West Broadway #1, New York, NY 10012

Typeset in 10/13pt Ehrhardt by Servis Filmsetting Ltd, Manchester
Printed in Great Britain by Cox & Wyman Ltd, Reading, Berks

contents

introduction

In 1992 I wrote a story called 'My father at Christmas'. The editor I sent it to said: 'I can't publish your piece as it arrived far too late for the Christmas issue. However I felt so sorry for you when I read it. I do hope your Christmases are better now.'

I was touched but surprised. I thought I had written a comic portrait of my eccentric father. But, without realizing it, I had exposed the darker aspects of Christmas known to many of us – the family tensions, individual loneliness in the midst of the festivities, the desperate need a child has for Christmas to live up to its expectations, frustration, despair and even death.

Too often, it seems, Christmas is a time of disappointment, seesawing emotions and valiant attempts to celebrate in the way expected by others. Escape from home and family is for some the best way of dealing with the annual trauma. Christmas tends to highlight human failure, material and spiritual. There is the real fear of not being able to provide adequate presents (or, as in some of these stories, the strain of adapting to Christmas from a different culture) and worse still, there is the failure to show love. Nowadays, with so many fragmented families, this is even more difficult. Of these eighteen stories, two deal with forgiveness, and three carry a message of hope. The original point of the Christian Christmas, to celebrate the day on which a saviour was born to help mankind, seems to have been lost. Only two stories touch on the birth of Christ. In this anthology death is more prevalent than birth.

However Christmas can also be experienced positively, as a catalyst, an occasion for self-examination, a period when things come to a head or when an intense or traumatic past experience is relived and finally understood.

The trouble is, we're supposed to be happy at Christmas. How difficult this is, particularly in December, when we often have some of the worst weather and the darkest and shortest days!

I personally would rather give Christmas a miss and read, or write, about it instead. I hope you enjoy these stories.

Elisa Segrave

a neck like yours

omar sattaur

By the beginning of December the back of the mail-order catalogue was usually missing in action or severely wounded. Rafeek and I would spend hours thumbing through its pages, trying to decide which of the newest toys and games to put on our Christmas lists. We'd group them into toys we wanted but knew our parents couldn't or wouldn't buy; those they might buy as a special present if we campaigned hard enough; and smaller, cheaper toys that we knew would be ours for the asking. But it was the first group that possessed us. In the lead up to Christmas 1967 I had my eye on a red, remote-controlled, battery-operated Porsche and Rafeek had his on a toy air rifle, a sort of glorified popgun.

I would stare so hard at the colour pictures that they became almost three dimensional. My nights were filled with dreams of manœuvring the red Porsche through a maze of chair legs in the sitting room. At times the flex that connected the car to the battery box with the tiny steering wheel on top would disappear altogether. I would be in the Porsche, dreaming at once of the view from the windscreen and of seeing the wheels turning, as if from a running board.

Daddy hated Christmas. He never bought presents but left it to Ma to choose them, wrap them and sign his name on the tags. We were not Christian, he would remind us, nor was there any reason, given our usual thrift, to suddenly throw caution to the wind just because the hawkers were shouting louder than usual. Ma, on the other hand, looked at Christmas as a chance to measure just how much of a family we were. Her ideal family was like a tapestry of images she'd plucked from the films that were on TV every year: *A Christmas Carol*, *To Kill a Mockingbird*, *David Copperfield* and *Tom Sawyer*. It made me sad to see her enthusiastic weaving in tatters by Boxing Day, but she'd start again the next year, hopeful as ever.

Ma would begin to prepare for Christmas in the spring; it was then that she soaked the dried fruits in sherry for the black cake, the rich Caribbean cake that we looked forward to eating at Christmas, weddings and other family celebrations. She would fill large brown bottles with the mashed fruit and hide them in a corner of the larder until it was time to bake the cake in December. 'How you does always give he the best bowl to lickle?' Rafeek would complain. 'You know Adam is the smallest,' Ma would reply, explaining nothing, but with a cadence that discouraged discussion. 'And it's lick, not lickle!' I would then take my time to lick the bowl and, when Ma wasn't looking, taunt Rafeek with fingers coated in the fruity, eggy mixture.

Daddy worked nights as a security guard and tried, mostly unsuccessfully, to sleep during the day. He was grumpy at the best of times but, by November, his grumpiness would become more focused – Christmas became a prime target. Ma would put flowers in a small vase on the TV. Daddy would remove them. 'You know how much this TV set cost, woman? You want to spoil the wood?'

'Is just some flowers Ali. Is just to make the place look nice.'

'It don't need no damn flower. Flower and current don't mix. You want blow up the TV set?' The flowers were plastic but Ma did not answer him.

We had lived only five years in Britain; the TV was a yardstick for progress. Aunty Pearly, Ma's cousin, did not have one even though she had been a decade in London. She hated Christmas too, but for different reasons. Pearly's husband had left her as soon as he knew his way around the bus and underground system so, after we'd arrived in London, Aunty Pearly spent her holidays with us.

She would pour scorn on the TV but never miss a viewing session.

The evening news was Daddy's favourite programme and he always watched it before leaving for work. We had to be absolutely silent throughout and then there'd be a film or drama series, much more to our liking. Daddy was allowed to talk through such unimportant programmes. At Christmas, Aunty Pearly was with us and his chat would often be directed to her.

'Eh eh, Pearly girl, like you don't want sleep tonight?'

'Is Christmas. I must spend some time with my cousin, not so Amna?'

Ma usually stayed out of these conversations.

'Oh, so is not the TV set that catch you eye?'

'TV set?' she sucked her teeth, 'when me mind tell me I could jus' lef' it an' sleep.'

'Pearly. I never once see you leave it. You know, I believe you would like a TV set more than a man.'

'You right there. You think I want a good-for-nothin' man who go drink rum day an' night an' spen' out all me hard-earn money? Eh, eh! Better I spen' it on a holiday back home than on any TV set. They does only show a lot of rubbish anyhow.'

'An' how Pearly love all that rubbish, eh?' In truth, Aunty Pearly was most quiet when the TV was on. When it was off she spent her time reminiscing about her deserting husband.

Rafeek and I prayed hard in the lead up to that Christmas. Rafeek wanted to join the army and, if there was a God, surely He could see how important it was for him to learn how to shoot straight from an early age? I hadn't decided yet whether I wanted to be a racing-car driver or a petrol-pump attendant – they both held a certain fascination for me. The important thing was to get the Porsche and the air rifle, so we concentrated all our willpower on that. I even tried buttering up Aunty Pearly.

'Aunty, why they does call you Pearly?' I had asked her many times before and knew how much she liked to tell me the answer. Rafeek was now jeopardizing the whole strategy by making stupid faces and miming her reply to me, behind her back.

'Well. You too small to remember your Uncle Zeek. He was a proper handsome man. He used to wear he moustache like Clark Gable and drive around on a big motorbike.'

'Who's Clark Nable?' Rafeek piped up.

'Gable boy, not Nable. Is a big American flim star. Anyway, your uncle love me so much he used to say a neck like mine deserve a pearl necklace. Yes, it was your Uncle Zeek who start callin' me Pearly.' Rafeek was making such violent retching motions behind her that Aunty Pearly caught him and gave him a hard slap on his bottom. 'You take you eyes and pass me, no? I go tar you behind for you, you little bitch.'

'Pearl necklace my backside,' Rafeek said after Aunty Pearly had made a dignified exit. 'Last time it was because her eyes was like two small pearls in pools of water. If he love her so much why would he run away, eh?'

That Christmas seemed never to arrive. The snow came just in time, a fortnight before the big day, temporarily taking our minds off cars and rifles. Our shoes had slippery soles but this only added to the thrill of sliding rather than walking. We had races to see who could skid the farthest. We chose the lamp post a few yards before the gate of our house as a landmark from which to start the slide. We took it in turn to run on tiptoe to the lamp post before breaking into a skid. One day, Rafeek had gone first, skidded, stopped expertly and turned in his tracks to mark the place and to watch my effort. I was determined to beat him. I took a deep breath and ran as fast as I could. I could barely keep balance but grinned at Rafeek as I saw his feet rush past. I was still grinning at him when I crashed into a pair of highly polished, brown brogues.

I was on my back, the snow wet and cold on my left thigh, staring up at a tall, portly Indian man with a black hat, a silver-tipped walking cane and a long, black winter coat.

'Hey, watch where you're going.' He grabbed hold of my arm and pulled me up. He had wide, thick lips and the long, wavy hair that leaked out of the sides of his black hat was streaked with grey. I don't think I'd ever seen anyone taller than Daddy before. I wriggled free and ran back to Rafeek. The stranger stood looking at our house. I could sense Rafeek's fear as the stranger turned towards us.

'Don't be frightened. Are you hurt?' Rafeek held my hand tightly.

'He's all right mister.' We ran hand in hand past him to our front gate.

'You live here? Come boys, don't be frightened.' His voice was deep. He spoke with a clear Caribbean accent, but it was very different from the ones we knew.

'Yes, this is . . .' I began when Rafeek jabbed me sharply in the ribs.

'Why you want to know where we live for?' Rafeek glared at him.

'I can see you are a smart boy. Your father is Ali, Murad Ali from La Penitence, isn't that so?'

'Come Adam,' Rafeek was giving nothing away.

'Look son,' the stranger said, buttoning up his enormous great-coat, 'I only want to know . . .' But we had already reached the front door and we could hear Ma's heavy footstep. We tumbled inside and when we turned and looked back, the stranger had gone.

'OK, OK, what's the big hurry?' I opened my mouth to speak when I felt a sharp blow to my shin.

'Nothin' Ma,' Rafeek said and bundled me upstairs. We were just inside our bedroom when I jumped on him and began hammering him with clenched fists.

'Wait, you stupid fool,' he was grinning at me. 'I didn' mean to hurt you but you keep blurting everything out. How do we know who that man is? You want us to get a lickin' for talking to strangers?'

'But it wasn't our fault.'

'You try explainin' that,' Rafeek said wisely. 'We'll watch out for him every day. He might be a thief-man. An' then we'll tell Daddy and Daddy go lick him good.'

'He's bigger than Daddy.'

'He might be bigger but he's all fat. Daddy got muscle.'

The sitting room was across the landing from ours, its bay window overlooking the front garden. We were up early next morning peering through the curtains to see if the stranger in the black hat was there. We looked that evening too, but he didn't show up. We kept the vigil for two whole days but the stranger stayed away. We went back to thumbing through the mail-order catalogue.

'If I get this rifle, we wouldn't have to worry about people like that fat man,' Rafeek said.

'You can't just shoot people Rafeek.'

'Oh no? I wouldn't even have to shoot anybody. They'd see the rifle and no thief-man would dare to come to we house. An' if they did then I'd shoot. First I'd shoot off his hat.'

Ma broke Rafeek's violent reverie by snatching the catalogue away. 'I tell you enough times. Stop manhandling the book. Look how all you destroying it. Leave it now an' help me put up the tree.'

We thought she'd never ask. Rafeek brought the cardboard box with the plastic tree down from the attic and I got the fairy lights and the decorations from the sideboard, downstairs in the dining room. The tinsel was in tatters and the baubles had lost some of their coloured coatings but the excitement they gave out tingled up my spine and made me want to dance. 'How many more days to Christmas, Ma?' I shouted.

'How many times you goin' to ask me the same question, Adam? How many was it yesterday?'

'Eight.'

'So how many from today?'

'Seven. But you goin' to buy me the Porsche, Ma?'

'Poach? What Poach?'

'You are. You are. You are.'

'I didn' say anything of the sort. But you better behave anyway or you won't get any present at all.'

By the time Daddy woke up, ate and came up to watch the news, the tree was up in the bay window and the fairy lights were twinkling, but with a clumsy twinkle, blinking abruptly, as if they didn't mean to. Daddy switched the light on and the Christmas tree lights off.

'What happen? Like you don't like to see the place looking nice?'

'That is a lot of pagan rubbish. An' anyway you only puttin' it up an' showin' off for the neighbours' sake. What I want with a blasted tree wastin' current day an' night.'

'You lie. I don't put it on whole night, just a little in the evenin's.'

Daddy noticed that the flowers had reappeared on the TV and demoted them to the floor, next to the wastepaper basket. 'I tell you not to put this blasted nonsense on the TV set.'

'Man, sometimes you is like a animal. You don't like nothin' nice.'

'That's right. I is a animal. You just carry on with you nonsense. You advertise to everybody in London that we got Christmas tree. The next thing you know, thief-man go break through you precious bay window.'

'We saw him Daddy,' I blurted, this time before Rafeek could stop me.

'Who, Adam? You see who?'

'We see the thief-man, he was big, big with a hat an' he had a big stick an' he nearly beat me an' Rafeek with it.'

'What? He nearly beat you? Where you see this man?'

'He lyin'. He didn' beat us Daddy, but he was outside the house the other day. We didn't see him any more,' Rafeek said, scowling at me. Ma and Daddy exchanged glances, but said nothing.

Aunty Pearly arrived early on Christmas Eve. She was wearing some sort of woollen balaclava and was breathing hard, her breath making clouds of steam that seemed to fill the porch with faint smells of rose-water and lemon. She kicked the doorstep to loosen the packed snow from the soles of her plastic boots with the fake fur lining. She had a heavy holdall in one hand and a net shopping bag in the other. 'Happy Christmas, Amna girl.' Ma handed Rafeek the holdall and me the shopping bag. As they hugged and kissed each other we ran up to the sitting room and rifled the shopping bag. The presents were wrapped in last year's paper, the frayed edges inexpertly trimmed. Excitement died quickly.

'A book for me and chocolate for you,' Rafeek reported after weighing the packages and holding them up to the light. We put the presents in the sitting room wall cupboard where all presents were 'hidden' until the morning of Christmas Eve, and her holdall in the spare room. Then we ran down to give her the obligatory kiss.

Aunty Pearly and Ma began to prepare the Christmas dishes. They began to skin an enormous pile of garlic for the garlic mutton. They peeled potatoes and onions and prepared a paste of garlic and ginger for the meat that Daddy was out buying. The house smelled of festivity. They began to reminisce of Christmases passed in Guyana. This inevitably drew memories of Uncle Zeek from Aunty Pearly's willing lips.

'He was good when he was sober, Amna. But when he was sweet with rum he was different man.'

'Is so they stay,' Ma's voice dropped to a circumspect whisper. 'When Ali was young he could proper drink rum. One time he had the nerve to bring he fancy woman into the house an' expect me to serve them. I jus' tek the cutlass and chase the two of them out the house. You should have do the same thing with Zeek.' Ma took the lid off a big pot of boiling rice and gave it a stir. Clouds of steam filled the kitchen.

'If I could have do that girl, I would. But I always thought that whatever Zeek do, an' however bad he behave, he would always come back home to me.'

Rafeek dragged me out of the kitchen to play in the front garden. We scraped the walls clean of snow and began to build an igloo around us. Its wall was about a foot high when we ran out of snow. I opened the gate to scrape some more off the pavement when I saw the large brown brogues again. I opened my mouth to shout for Rafeek but no sound came out. I need not have feared, though, for the stranger took no notice of us this time. He was looking down the passage at the side of the house, concentrating on our kitchen window. By the time I could run back and close the gate the stranger was already walking hurriedly away. We both ran inside the house, up to the sitting room and pulled the net curtains from the bay window. We just caught a glimpse of the black hat and greatcoat before the stranger turned the corner. We ran into the wall cupboard where the presents were 'hidden'.

'Look. We got to keep a lookout day an' night now. Tomorrow is Christmas an' we don't want no thief-man breaking in.' It was then that I saw a present that neither of us had seen before. I jammed my thumb into Rafeek's ribs. 'Look, it's the gun, it's the gun.' Rafeek looked at the tall slim package. It was the right height, the right weight. His jaw dropped and his voice became a whisper.

'Hey, Adam. You want to see it?'

'You mad or what. We goin' to get catch. Then it's big trouble.'

'You would get catch. Not me. Look, it's easy. All we got to do is sneak in here tonight when they all sleepin'. Jus' to take a look an' wrap it back. Nobody goin' to know nothin'.'

'I don't know . . .'

'You chicken. You yellabelly, chickenshit . . .'

'You shut up. All right, all right. I goin' to come with you.'

The day dragged interminably on. Daddy arrived at about lunchtime with a big bag of meat, fresh from the halal butchers in Dalston Lane. 'How is it Pearly? You find a man yet?' It was one of Daddy's common greetings to Aunty Pearly.

'I need a man like I need my foot chop off. I perfectly happy livin' alone. In any case, Zeek was the only man for me, an' he gone to make money in Dubai.'

'Gone to make money? I thought he gone to make honey.'

'Just shut up Ali. You does only think the worst of everybody. Zeek was a good man an' a lovin' husban' to me, you hear!'

'Only jokin' Pearly dear. Don't overheat.'

Aunty Pearly seemed especially sentimental that Christmas. That evening she came upstairs and caught Rafeek and me flipping the pages of the mail-order catalogue. Rafeek had borrowed Ma's tape measure and was taking note of the dimensions of the air rifle given in the blurb. He was about to measure the tall box in the wall cupboard when Aunty Pearly packed the catalogue away, turned the TV off and brought out her photo album to show us.

'You know who is this, Adam?' she said, pointing to a good-looking man with a 1940s moustache. 'Clark Nable,' Rafeek answered, stupidly. 'That's your uncle Zeek,' Aunty Pearly said, ignoring him. It was a black and white photograph with serrated edges, turned yellow with age. On the facing page was a picture of Clark Gable, cut out from a film magazine with colours in his cheeks and lips that were larger than life. Daddy had appeared in his easy chair without us noticing.

'Those were the days, eh Pearly?' he said. Aunty Pearly went very quiet. Suddenly she snapped the album shut and walked quickly to her room. 'Eh, eh! What happen with she? I say anything bad to she?' We knew we were not supposed to answer such questions. Rafeek had moved over to the window, and was calling me over. 'I see the man,' he whispered excitedly. But, by the time I reached the window, the stranger had turned the corner.

'Which man?' Daddy asked, but we both raced out of the room and down the stairs.

Nine thirty, and bedtime, arrived at last. Ma even commented on our lack of protest about going to bed. We got between our sheets and I tried with all my might to stay awake. But my eyelids kept dropping, heavily. Every time I fell asleep Rafeek would shout a whispered: 'Adam! You little pussyfoot. Wake up. You have to keep awake!' We talked until about ten o'clock and then his words became part of my dreams. I had long run out of things to say. Rafeek hit on another idea. He held my left hand in his right and, whenever I dropped off, he would raise my arm up and down a few times. But it didn't work. My eyes refused to stay open and after a while I slept soundly until he woke me, I don't recall how long after.

'Quick. Let's go,' he whispered, 'they're all in bed.' I can't remember saying anything at all. I could barely stand as Rafeek dragged me out of bed, the heaviness of sleep holding me back and pulling me downwards. It was only the cold floor on the soles of my feet that kept me awake enough to walk. All was quiet. Daddy was downstairs in the dining room next to the kitchen. He often read the papers there when he was on holiday and couldn't adjust to the changed sleeping times. Rafeek led me into the sitting room. The Christmas lights were on, filling the room with their clumsy twinkle of coloured light. We stumbled into the wall cupboard, Rafeek chiding me in whispers to keep quiet. He found the tall, cardboard box and was carefully lifting the sticky tape, trying not to tear the wrapping paper, when we heard a loud knock on the door.

'Who . . .,' I managed to let out before Rafeek slapped a hand across my mouth to silence me. We were both trembling with fear. I could feel Rafeek's chest heaving against the back of my head until we realized that the knock came from downstairs.

'It's somebody at the front door,' Rafeek whispered, 'come an' look.'

We tiptoed to the bay window and looked down. It was the stranger with the hat. He was giving Daddy something. Their voices were murmurs but we could make out that the man was in a hurry. They embraced and the stranger left. We could hear the front door closing and Daddy's heavy footstep coming up the stairs. We were in bed before he reached the top of the stairs but neither of us could sleep for a while. Even Rafeek couldn't understand how Daddy knew the thief.

Ma woke us and let us open some small presents of sweets before breakfast, just to keep us quiet. Nat King Cole was singing *Rambling Rose* and the tree was blinking. Ma had decorated the TV with a new set of plastic flowers in a fluted, bottle green vase. Outside, the snow had not yet melted. We looked out of the window and imagined that we saw the big imprints of brogues on the front doorstep. A sharp, brief fear rose in my chest as I remembered the night's events.

We knew nothing could happen until after breakfast so we ran into Aunty Pearly's bedroom to wake her. Daddy was fast asleep and best left like that until Ma told us to wake him. That was not usually until the coffee was poured and the breakfast on the table. He was an impatient man. That day, just thinking of him and the stranger frightened me, so I stayed well away from his bedroom door.

Christmas for us children finally arrived when the last piece of toast was swallowed and the dishes cleared from the table. We tore upstairs and sat waiting for Aunty Pearly – she was always cast in the role of Santa for some reason – to give out the presents. Rafeek got his air rifle and I got my Porsche from Ma and Daddy. I'm not sure whether it was as exciting as the pictures at the back of the catalogue. From Aunty Pearly, Rafeek got a book and I got a bar of chocolate. Rafeek was usually right in his guesses. Ma got a box of chocolates from us, a bottle of scent from Daddy and a slip from Aunty Pearly. Daddy got aftershave from us, a wash bag from Ma and a tie from Aunty Pearly. It could have been just like any other Christmas. But then Daddy produced a small, oblong present wrapped in shiny gold paper and held it in front of Aunty Pearly.

'And a special one for you, Father Christmas.' Aunty Pearly was momentarily speechless.

'Ali? What come over you man? You shouldn't have bothered with me.'

'I didn't,' Daddy said, a little callously, I later thought. 'Somebody you know brought it by late last night.' Aunty Pearly's fingers were trembling as she carefully unfolded the gold paper. She gasped as her eyes fell on the string of pearls in the black velvet case.

'He didn't want to stay, Pearly,' Daddy said, more gently than I'd ever heard him speak to Aunty Pearly before.

the snowbird

a. l. kennedy

They were fascinated. It wasn't his fault, their fault, anyone's fault.
No one to shout at and no one to blame. There was just some quality
about it that tugged their imaginations away from anything else he
could offer – snowbirds and firemen, Santa Claus and earthquakes,
they, each of them, failed completely to be of interest.

'How about I read you something?'

'No. Tell us what you did today.'

'I could tell you about the snowbird that comes in the night and
shines like glass, like glass full of rainbows in the dark, all of himself.
He makes the frost on the windows out of snow glass. Um, I could
tell you about . . . that.'

'Tell us what you did with the boxes. Were you in the boxes
today?'

'The love boxes.' Sarah, getting it wrong on purpose which she
could sometimes like to do.

'They're glove boxes. Glove. And I did what I did with them yesterday, all over again today. Nothing special. They're never special.'

'Please.'

'Go on, Dad.'

'No, you go on now. If you can't be sensible then I'll get cross.
And it's too late. You should be asleep.'

'Oh, Dad.'

'You always say we should be sleeping when you don't want to
talk.' There was nothing arrogant in the way she said that, no edge

that he could feel. She might have been noting her temperature, or the time.

'Why can't you just be good. Why can't you just for once be good. Every time, when you're back from your mother it's like this. I mean, what are you trying to tell me? Do you want to stay with her? Is that what you want? You can tell me?' That wasn't a question, why did it come out like a question? He was losing grip of his inflection. 'Well, tell me. If it is.'

Without warning, he was on the edge of tears, lowering his head to massage his eyes, knowing they were too wet not to be noticed. The sisters looked up at him the way they generally did, neither alarmed nor embarrassed, only very still. Patient, that's what they were, patient. Amanda and Sarah staring, with their sympathetic, clear sad eyes, as if they were women, hiding in behind girl's faces. Because he had never been anything better than a child in his life and so they were growing to be his sisters, not his daughters. They were pushing aside time so that he wouldn't be lonely, so that he could talk to them. Rely on them.

No, that was only his thinking. He felt guilty because they mattered to him and he wanted to do his best. He should remember that. Truthfully, he was not guilty. Perhaps uncomfortable would be a better word. His daughters made him uncomfortable. No more than that.

'Daddy, do you have a headache?'

'Sssh, yes he's got one.'

'Don't talk about me as if I'm not here.'

They blinked, almost flinched while he shouted. They were such flowers really, it made him breathless inside to think of the damage he might do them and not know. He mustn't forget that he was still bigger than they were, louder and more frightening. He must be nourishing. With them, their mother would be catty, competitive, female and he must be her antidote. He dabbed their heads with his fingertips, kissed his hands and dabbed again.

'I'm sorry for shouting. That was wrong. Yes, my head hurts.'

'Will I get you some water with pills in?' Amanda diving into practicalities with a smooth, calm nod.

She was wasted on her generation – should have been a refugee, evacuee, the smile to keep your spirits up, adrift in the open boat. He often wondered how she would manage to rest here contented in such unchallenging surroundings and saw her grown up and protesting and debating and migrating and dispensing courage over-seas. Then again, how long would her home stay civilized, soft. She had almost a lifetime to live, should have a lifetime to live, and things would change here, were already turning savage, making the news-papers seem foreign, a daily fear.

'How many has he had already. Of the pills.'

'No, ask him.'

'How many pills have you had already, Dad. To make sure you're not over dose.'

'Overdosed. That's the word, he told us, you remember.'

They watched his mouth, ready to understand any slowness, sadness, angriness. He had made them understanding in all of the wrong ways. Sarah was holding Amanda's hand and they sat, per-fectly still, as if they had been cut from paper and then folded open into two little children of equal solemnity.

'All right.'

It was Sarah's turn to bring him the glass. It was carefully half full and carried in both her hands like a present or a dove, its water still fizzing slightly with painkiller.

'Mind the water, Dad. Outside is making the pipes go frosty, will they burst?'

'No, I don't think so.' He swallowed his first mouthful trying not to show the flicker of pain at his nervous tooth.

'Is it too cold? Amanda could put in some hot. From the kettle, not the tap.' Amanda had told her about the dangers of lead in the pipes and boiling kettles. She trusted Amanda. More than she trusted him? Differently, just differently.

'No, it's not too cold. It's fine.' Say thank you always, so that they will. 'Thank you.'

'It's our pleasure.'

He watched them nod and move to the stairs. They would get

themselves ready for bed now, brushing their teeth together –
Amanda behind Sarah because she was tallest, both of them spitting
neatly when necessary and then cleaning the bowl. They would wash
thoroughly, leaving each other alone for the private things and
having their own odd organizations for who went first. Sometimes,
up there, they would laugh. He had no idea why.

When they needed to be tucked in, they would call him.

The telephone rang and his hand jerked in response, slewing
water out of the glass and down his shirt. That would be their
mother.

'Yes, they're fine. Just getting ready for bed.'

Except they would be listening now, getting ready but collecting
every word, not forgetting the pauses.

'It was time for them to go to bed, that's why they're going to bed.
If you want to speak to them, they can still come down. I didn't know
you were going to ring.'

'No, I couldn't have guessed.'

'Will I call them –'

'I'll call –'

Now she will talk about your job which means about money and
her house which means money and the swarms of bad habits she
imagines you have fallen into without her, which means about
money which you spend unwisely. Perhaps you lie about when she
isn't watching, smoking, the three of you together – looking at
wicked comics, turning on the television and letting it say what it
says at your daughters without even intervening to point out what a
poisonous kind of sump it is. It is an electric cesspool, should throw
it away, push your foot through it if this wouldn't cause a potentially
hazardous explosion.

He wishes she would not talk about his job because of how this
makes him feel. His job does not give him safe ground to stand on –
she can score points without even knowing why the weakness she
finds is there.

'Of course I'm getting them presents. It's Christmas. I've got
them presents.'

'You can buy them whatever you like.'

Keep our responsibilities nicely separate, there.

'Me? Nothing special. I'm not good at thinking – they tell me. Just useful things, clothes, that's what they asked for. And a stuffed dog, puppy kind of thing. Sarah wanted a penny whistle, Christ knows where you get them.'

Trying to keep it bottled, the way her voice made him feel. He shouldn't be annoyed because she would like that. He shouldn't be annoyed because the girls wouldn't. He felt squeezed between them.

'I know, I know that. You can still buy her piano lessons. I don't think a whistle will stop her playing the piano, I think she's musical. You can't carry a piano about, can you? Maybe that's why . . .'

'Look, I don't mind. Ask them, they know more than me.'

Now she'll pull something. Every Christmas, she tries something. More often than that, but particularly at Christmas. Why do people do that? Families, everyone tearing each other apart just at the thought of being together, never mind on the day. Why at Christmas?

'If you wanted them to put up the decorations, they could have done it tonight.'

'What do you mean. How not ready could they be.'

She wasn't going to have them again, take them away. Tomorrow lunchtime, their school would give them up to him for the whole of the holiday – the three of them on holiday at once which was difficult, a whole year's miracle, to arrange – and she wouldn't get them again, not until Boxing Day. She'd had them at Christmas last year and now it was his turn.

Not that it mattered. None of it mattered, all of this stuff just descending into incredible pettiness, but it only took one person to get petty and then you would both have to be petty or you would lose – the cunt would wipe her shoes on your face, in your mouth. Bad word. Shouldn't think cunt. Their mother, that's what she was. Their mother. Bad mother. But their mother.

'Daddy?'

Were they calling down to save him? Were they worried? Did they just want him because they wanted him?

'I'm on the phone to your mother. Hold on a minute. Is it an emergency?'

'Just that we're going to sleep.'

'We're in bed, we're not asleep yet.' Amanda, she liked to correct, get one over on big sister. You could sneak her into talking that way, if she was having a sulk, just say something inaccurate and she couldn't resist pulling you up. No getting away from reality with her around. Very like her mother.

'I'll be up any minute. Look, I have to go. I thought we had this all agreed –'

'Well –'

'Well –'

He really would shout, if he couldn't push his way in here. It was always more difficult, breaking her flow when you couldn't see her. And she knew it.

'I will have to go because they are shouting me but I will call you again tomorrow if thats all right fine goodbye then.' Not leaving a toe hold to kick her way in. Petty, petty, petty. But she started it. True.

'Daddy?'

'On my way. Feeling much better now. No headache. Thanks for the pills. On my way.'

They'll know. They'll look at the way you're walking, the closed smile on your face and they'll know it didn't go too well. People should be able to suspend what they do for children, to grow past them and get safe away. Why give two girls such a terrible idea of what a relationship could be? Maybe they wouldn't even enjoy Christmas, would associate it with arguments and turn to other religions in later life, how could you predict?

He would wash his hands and face before he saw them, give himself a good all over scrub and pretend he was checking they'd left the bathroom tidy.

'I'll take you for your shoes tomorrow, if you'd like that.'

'You could wait until afterwards and then there would be sales.'

Amanda saying it and meaning it, but not seeing Sarah's eyes. She still wanted presents on the proper day. Then Boxing

Day ones from her mother, that part must be quite nice, really.

Why the Hell did their mother want them to go over and decorate her house? She surely wouldn't want all that nonsense for the sake of one day and then just have it hanging round. He couldn't imagine anyone wanting to decorate for only themselves. She would go into a depression and end up phoning the girls, crying, making those acid promises. Leaving him the threats.

'What are you thinking about, Dad?'

'Oh, bits and bobs. What do you want for Christmas dinner?'

'Well . . .' very cautious, 'Mum said she was getting us turkey so maybe we should have beef.'

'Or pork is nice.'

What a good idea – makes you wonder who put it there. So she was having the fucking turkey. It didn't matter. He didn't like turkey. It only had an effect because it was some kind of peculiar victory. Probably, she was over there, right now, keeping score, making her winning advantage secure.

'Whichever you want. We could have beans on toast.'

'No.' Sarah could not imagine Christmas with beans on toast, it was too horrible to joke about.

'All right, we'll decide tomorrow when we're out and order ourselves a nice cow or a pig.'

'Or both.'

Yes, but there was no need to overdo it. He had the feeling Amanda would be vegetarian by next year, she had that kind of mind.

'And now you can tell us about the glove boxes. You promised.'

'Oh, no. I didn't promise at all.'

'Tell us.'

'And then we'll go to sleep.'

So admit defeat because it has been a long day and the days will get even longer before everything of this is over and the new year has arrived and is already dull.

'I worked in the glove boxes today –'

'In the citadek?'

'In the Citadel. I worked with the glove boxes and with the big black gloves so that none of the bad stuff would get out. Like the glass box with those rats they had on television.'

'OH. You haven't got rats, have you.'

'No, we don't have rats.'

'Good.'

'Come on, we've got an early start in the morning, lots to do. And I want to take a bath before I go to bed.'

'You like baths, don't you?'

'Yes, I like baths.'

You can say that because it's true.

You can say that because you would love to climb into the bath with no lights on and see nothing of yourself, feel nothing of yourself, be washed away.

You can say that because another container spilled today and filled the Citadel with something you can only imagine as very fine glass needles, flying and burrowing. You have heard things about the glove boxes, their safety, the invisible sparks they let slip to sink under your skin and burn through the codes that make you yourself. You could be changing all the time and this is too small for you to feel, impossible for you to see, only poorly translated into a colour change in your indicator badge, a decontamination or two. But how can they clean away something that has made itself a part of you and is waiting to tell you its time.

You don't know what you bring them back from the Citadel, a little more each day. The weightless sightless something you could be breathing into your former wife, pressing into the hands of your properly registered childminder, stepping into the pile of your carpet, hugging into the hearts of your daughters' bones.

You should be apart from them, kept away in case of accident. Unless the accident has already happened in their air or their water, they maybe have eaten their death in spite of you, or walked through it on the way to school. You live too close to the Citadel here. At night it shines through the town like a big, nasty eye and you wish it had never been thought of. None of it should exist.

Diseases can be triggered psychologically, you know that, which is why you must, most of the time, not think. You take baths. You don't want to hurt anybody.

'We like them, too.'

'Sorry?'

'We like baths.'

Their skin has an almost glow about it, a blue, Celtic sheen they have from their mother who could never and probably still cannot go out in the sun. They are snow children, happy and safe in winter. You wish it would snow for them because they would like that and anywhere will look better in snow, even the Citadel. Although that is always snowed over somehow, hard to look at and really see, difficult to contemplate. You imagine it sometimes like a black umbrella opening inside your head and then turn away from it again.

'Good, good. Girls, how do you like being at your mother's? Is it all right?'

'All right.' Sarah speaking quite clearly, although she is almost asleep. She has the nicest voice of the whole family. You dream of her sometimes becoming a singer, an actress, newsreader, preacher – something lyrical and free.

'It's nice to be back home, though.'

'Much nicer.'

'Well, I'm glad you like it here.'

Tuck them in and leave them alone. Do not ask them questions they will not understand. Do not make them understand. Do not make them go away just because you are afraid.

'Go on then, Dad.'

'Mmh?'

'Your bath.'

'Yes. You sleep tight, then. Kisses on the heads and sleep tight. Call me, if you want something. Anything important. Night, night.'

And go and step into the water in the dark, feel it mouthing and nudging up, settling round your wrists and your neck as you sit and then lie. Open your eyes. Close them. No change.

glass cheques

andrew o'hagan

Every other morning, just after milk but before the start of painting, Tubs McAllister would raise his thick hand and whisper 'I'm needing'. Those on either side of him made faces, behind him they pegged their noses, and the rest of the class twisted from side to side clutching their throats, poking their tongues out, pretending to puke. Tubs, as his hand lifted off the desk to begin its sorry ascent, would have a beamer, a brasser, a burn-on, a reddy – would, whatever you call it, have a face so red, and so crumpled with bubbling tears, that he looked fit to burst open any second.

Mrs Curry would swoop in and hurry him out of the class. Though nobody felt for Tubs, everybody felt for her – holding the warm hand of the boy who always spoke too late, the shitey fatso, the one with the vile lump at the back of his shorts, the spaz, the spanner, the skittery dipstick Tubs McDumper. The auxiliary kept spare white pants in a tub at the back of the cloakroom though, sometimes, McAllister would mess himself so bad there'd be nothing to do but send him home.

'It's lava,' Catriona Kelly said on the fourth day of the new term, 'lava going down his legs.'

Mostly he'd go off on his own, his classmates craning their necks to watch him out the window as he went. There he'd go, down the school path, up over the railway bridge leading into the scheme, waddling along, legs apart, like a little cowboy bereft of his horse. The kids would fall about, and Mrs Curry would stand at the front of the class, thin-lipped, saying nothing.

Mrs Curry came just after the summer. They gave her three classes in one, three year groups in one class; and though her term in charge of them was cut short, she managed to build up a reputation for craziness, for neatness, for oddness and coolness, that – to some minds – had no rival in any other class or school or in any other time. Things started perfectly. From the very first ring of the morning bell, Mrs Curry, walking nimbly over the playing fields towards the hut that was to be her classroom, saw that everything would be just fine, that it could well be OK.

'Our new teacher's like a cartoon,' said Michael Elderley, spying her from the playground as she marched across the grass.

Curry was albino; the children in her class called her Beano. Everything in the hut was darker than her, including the milk by the door and the chalk in a saucer sat on a runner under the blackboard.

With her light hair, she looked like a papier-mâché angel whose mouth and eyes had been freshly drawn in with damp crayons. And she had one of the finest, by which people meant the thickest, moustaches ever sported by a lady teacher in East Kilbride. The sun glinted off it, the smaller kids thought it lovely: some of the boys were intrigued, they fancied her; the girls, the leading girls, rubbed furry pencil cases across their small mouths, wondering what it would be to be so fancied.

They all sat in rows, heads lolling on shrugging shoulders, whilst the great new Miss sounded out new words from a gap somewhere under that smouldering, smokey bush of a tash. A shushing, teaching thing, Beano stormed into the minds of her youngsters, filling corners which used to be happily dark, naming and placing furniture previously covered in white drape. She flooded them – and then left them before the year was out, by simply vanishing.

Beano's classroom was done up like some sort of palace in a watercoloured dream, inside a hut at the edge of the playing fields. She encouraged them to cover their jotters, squared ones and lined, with wallpaper and drawings so long as they wrote in their name, their class (P3-6) and the words St John-of-the-Cross R.C. The blue, wooden walls of the hut would rumble and creak at times of the day when trains went by, or when lorries and buses ran past on the road outside. It happened too when workers at a quarry on the other side of the bypass let off explosives to break up the ground. The hut was a thing in itself, a place apart from the rest of the school and the houses which lined up around it: it was their world, the children felt it was theirs, and Beano's first, unworried days were spent helping them celebrate the shapes and colours of their new freedom.

'Mint. Walk now children, between the desks, and think of smelling mint.'

'Mint Cracknel mint? The chocolatey mint? That kind Miss?' shouted Marie Nugent, walking the length of the back wall with her hands clapped over her eyes.

'Yes Marie, indeed,' she said, 'whatever kind of mint you see in your head, if you can see it, then go ahead and smell it too.'

Marie, with the rest of the class, went chewing and sniffing to the sound of Beano's semi-singing voice. Bumping this way and that, their nostrils flaring out to meet Beano's lovely-sounding smell, they eventually opened their eyes in turn to see their teacher standing on an upturned bucket out front, waving her arms around her head like someone lost in the conducting of a great orchestra.

The hut was smothered in trees; they grew up and along the side of the railway banking which bordered the east side of the school, their branches dipping down to the flat roof. Beano called it 'the tabernacle of your primary education, the seat of your learning'. Nobody knew what she was on about, though they liked the way she said it. She'd turn up the palms of her hands (one hand had a glove on it, the hand she used to write on the board with), she'd blink, and after a while her head would tremble, and then she'd say it, some-times twice, before telling them to get on with something quiet, something usually requiring paints. 'I'm stepping out for a moment. Stay silent,' she'd say. 'Just for now.' Then she'd go into the cup-board.

As the weeks went by Beano, having sparked everything off, saw less and less of the kids in their moments of discovery. She'd get them going then slip quietly into the cupboard. They got used to that. They'd fill their time doing up the hut; drawing out a thought and colouring it in with felt tips. With egg cartons and bin liners they invented a funny world; teaching themselves, for the most part, how to create and inhabit a place of their own making – a rare place, built up from snatches of time when Beano had stepped out.

'Mrs Curry said to use your fingers like your tongues, your tongue,' said Catriona to Mark Orr, who was messing about with Play-Doh, pushing it through the neck of a plastic bottle. 'We're too old now to roll it – Mrs Curry – but she said, she said to touch it and taste its colour but not to eat it Mark.'

Catriona Kelly loved bossing and telling the others what to do. She walked around talking and talking and saying 'Mrs Curry' and putting shells up to her ear when she couldn't think of another thing to say.

'Mrs Curry – you can hear the wind, whispering – Mrs Curry said – a story,' said Catriona, eating a chew and lying on the teacher's desk with the shell to her ear, balancing it there, without hands.

Everyone stuck painted card on the wall and wrote in their jotters. The hut was a tardis spinning through time, a space garden, an Indian reservation outside Glasgow, a street filled with customized trucks at the North Pole, a Chinese temple encrusted with egg-carton-dimple-shaped rubies. Only once, when a boy called Samson chipped a girl's ear with a ruler, did Beano lose the rag. She belted him with a borrowed strap, making him place one hand neatly under the other, and the sound of six heavy, nippy slaps filled the hut. She put him outside for an hour.

Outside it was cold, and he strolled over to the other side of the playing field. A horse called Dobbin stood by a hole in the railway fence; he fed it cold fistfuls of grass torn out of the field. He could see his own face, his face like a potato, bending up and down in the horse's watery eye. He stretched his palm out, with the grass on top, feeling the nice way the horse nudged its teeth and lips into the stinging cup of his hand. The others watched him from the window. He'd been belted.

After that, when Beano went into the cupboard (a thing she did more and more often) she'd hand her glove to one of the older boys, a boy with plenty of brothers – the Grimes – some who were known to run in gangs and deal stuff around the scheme. He'd been staying on in the hut after dark sometimes, just hanging around to talk with Beano. They called him The Boy David. His name wasn't David – it was Fergus – but they called him The Boy David after seeing a programme on TV about a Peruvian boy who was born with a funny mark in the middle of his face. Fergus only had a tiny mark, a birth mark, but the name got to him all the same. So there he was, The Boy David, standing in front of the class several times a day, and now and then turning to face the board. He'd pull the glove tighter before turning with the chalk. Someone had rifted or farted or shouted and that meant he'd to write up their name and the nature of the crime.

The coming on of Fergus, the funny-looker who became the Grass, was the start of the trouble in Beano's hut. He loved the job, he chalked his head off: every mutter and parp noted in the knowledge that Beano would slap or belt the guilty ones when she came out. Some of those named, staring at The Boy David with pleading, hateful eyes, would break down in the minutes before her return. Even McAllister – snottery, shitey Tubs McAllister – paid close attention when the child Fergus stood before the class, legs apart, arms folded, like the King of Siam.

They couldn't believe it. Something had gone wrong, Beano'd gone mad, everything changed quicker than they could say. In the run up to Christmas, just as there was a whole new seasonal world to paint, a chill set in. Beano was pacing inside the cupboard more than ever and The Boy David was on the rampage. Many of the kids couldn't think to draw, some just sat staring. Beano had started paying her deputy, giving him empty lemonade bottles – and not just lemonade, but Red Cola and Tizer – in return for his good work with the chalk. He always had one or two in his schoolbag. Kids who used to be pals with him were sick, ashamed; standing in the main yard at playtime they'd spit on the ground as he tripped past, empties clanking on his back.

'Any glass cheques?' they'd shout. 'Any bottles?'

Most of them, without saying it, felt that glass cheques – the returnables most people felt too embarrassed to return – were exactly the right kind of payment for a dick like Fergus, The Boy David, the ugly Peruvian who grassed on his mates.

In class Mrs Curry looked at Fergus with her watery, blinking, rose-coloured eyes as if there was some big joke going on that only they could get. They'd stare each other out, half-smiling, thinking the rest of them couldn't see. Him with his face, her with hers, stripping the very colour off the walls. Catriona started putting her head on the desk all the time, Marie Nugent kept having sore stomachs and wanting to go to the medical room and Michael Elderley just sat bored, trying to get his fingers stuck in a hole he'd worn out in the inside of his desk.

'We should treat each Christmas as if it was our very last,' said Beano one morning. This began a few days which were like the class's first days with Beano. McAllister hadn't dumped in class for three mornings running, Beano brushed up her hair 'in lieu of snow' and, for a reason nobody knew, The Boy David didn't get his hand in the glove so much, so was sulking over by the window. Something had happened. He hated the sound of the class, the sound of them getting excited and he hated Beano's laughter. Beano, the turncoat, had gone this way and that. He had his head leaning on the backs of his hands, his elbows propped on the desk, and with his fingers he secretly turned up the top lids of his eyes, pulling the skin up over the lashes so the red bits showed.

'Fucking freaky Beano-eyes,' he whispered to himself.

A plastic Santa was placed at the front of the class, on a board normally used for rolling Plasticine on, and everyone was asked to put their tuck money through a slot in its beard. As they did so, the children were told to send a prayer to Mary and think of how the 'blessed, black babies' would spend the money. Beano got everyone going. Rifling through coat pockets at home, going round the doors asking for money in the evenings, the kids looked to put colour back into their hut by pleasing the blessed gnome sat at the front of the class. The coins came in, and Beano set the count for 22 December.

An aeroplane, on its way to America, crashed into a street of houses not far away on the night before the count. In the morning, the younger group were full of questions and wanted to draw the news, but Mrs Curry just sat on a chair at the back, asking them to listen while she sang a hymn in praise of 'the people who fell from the sky'. Catriona Kelly said she'd make up a song for the people who died when the plane fell on top of them.

'Now they're in the sky,' she said.

'Who is? Who's in the sky?' asked Beano, looking up.

'The ones who weren't in the sky but were in the house. The plane came on top of them. Now, they are in the sky,' said Catriona, before asking if anyone had seen the picture of the upside-down woman, with her seat belt still on, sat on top of a chimney stack.

'Shush now,' warned Beano. 'Shush, and say your rosary while I step out. Be as quiet as you can.' The blood vessels glowed in her eyes, pinker than ever and wetter, as she slipped behind the cupboard door.

No one watched over the class as they said their rosary. McAllister, on the third Hail Mary of the second decade, quietly peed himself and had to wait, all wet, for twenty minutes till Beano came back in, and then another ten while she went searching for the tub of pants.

When they filed into the hut after lunchtime, Michael Elderley, cracking his fingers and whistling, was the first to notice that the Santa was missing. The Plasticine board was there, but no Santa. Beano exploded. They'd never seen her, never like this. Wild and in tears, she blamed everyone in turn; she was so angry that, for a second, a bit of red seemed to colour up her face. She shook some by the shoulders, poked at others, throwing pictures into the air, sand on to the floor, demanding that someone among them find the missing Santa. She'd gone all wrong. She took down the metal crucifix from the wall and toured it round the desks, making each of them kiss it and swear they didn't know the whereabouts of the money box. When she got to Fergus's desk, she lifted her head and hesitated. She offered him the crucifix and they stared long into each other's eyes.

'No Miss,' he said.

At least half the class, especially McAllister and the wee Primary Threes, cried and shook. Some of the older ones, the bigger girls, bit on their bottom lips and twisted their hair, feeling excited. Beano started hammering on his desk with the crucifix, each blow peeling another strip off the surface, revealing a much softer and cleaner wood underneath. She raised the cross over her head each time. Eventually, her teeth bared and her face glistening, she brought it down on his desk and held it there with both hands. He sniffed and turned away.

'Mrs Curry, you have the Santa,' he whispered to the wall.

She dragged his schoolbag from under his chair and threw it across the room, towards the corner, where it smashed down, the bottles inside breaking one on top of the other. Beano ran after them, panting, as if to get at them before they hit the floor. Then she leant against the door, holding on to herself, her expression blurred and amazed.

The Boy David walked over to the cupboard, turned the door handle, and pushed the door forward as far as it would go. Those tall enough could see in. The top shelves had one or two piles of jotters and a few flat boxes of pencils. But the lower shelf had nothing on it but a few short bottles – bottles of Temazepam – around which lay dozens of squeezed-out capsules, some of them strewn over the floor looking like crushed, sun-dried beetles. There was a length of flimsy rubber pipe and some other things wrapped in a length of moist cotton wool. The liquid innards of the capsules, the little that remained, sat in a tiny metal dish shaped like a kidney.

The Boy David strolled in and lifted a black handbag off a hook, bringing it out and placing it on the teacher's table. Many of those in tears couldn't work it out: they were crying about the Santa, or was it the plane crash or the sight of the altered Mrs Curry, now staring at the floor, her face so white against the hut's linoleum; Mrs Curry, who'd so suddenly, so certainly stopped liking them? Fergus lifted the bag upside down and let the things inside fall on to the table. The Santa eased out slowly; a black stopper on its base popped and coins spilled over the desk and on to the floor. Fergus picked up the glove and the chalk and wrote the words 'Curry does jellies Beano is a junky I saw her'.

The hut was noiseless till McAllister, quietly at first but with a sound that steadily rose, began to chuckle deep into a clenched fist. When the class turned their heads from the board their teacher had gone.

a difference made

kelvin christopher james

Harsh terrain it was, with stark burnished rocks and dry gravelly soil that rattled downwards when the cold wind gusted. The scant ground vegetation was wizened, bearing prickles, and spines, and sharp spicules. The larger plant life contraried gravity, leaning into the blow. Sheer hillsides, the skeletons of millennia, bared roots searching enormously deep through the stony loam for grudging sustenance.

For one moon, proceeding with the integrating machine, the seeker AnsienRa had warily scouted the range, examining the vitality, isolating the most sophisticated drives, before determining that those human were best choice. Social creatures, the human species seemed to enjoy seven or so organ-associated basic senses. And beyond these gifts, humans apparently possessed numerous higher, emotion-driven senses which sometimes mingled into multitudes of finer nuances.

But AnsienRa could learn only so much by external observation: for closer perspective, the seeker needed to cross over within a basic human, one with complete feeling and a manageable brain. Through phases of a second moon, eager to touch and test otherness, the seeker endlessly strove the machine towards a mind matchable, a one efficient, and with full force of humanity.

All the while, the machine returned, 'Be patient and provide fit subject,' and in careful manner, monitored and encouraged AnsienRa to range them near a valley and set ambush. Until, in time, an appropriate soul blundered along, and the machine advised, 'This one suffices. Bring us to working proximity.'

AnsienRa swiftly complied, and from the plain radiance of the machine's pulsing, became certain of near interface with true feeling, and reasoned for haste, 'O most efficient machine, you will share all this gestalt the sooner we three become one. Is this not so?'

Then, as the machine acquiesced and allowed complicity, AnsienRa became less seeker and more human, finally achieving every seeker's unequaled bliss – a mental symbiont, a perfect witness. But the sudden exhilaration of knowing in this bizarre, human manner overwhelmed, and set down AnsienRa to grovel in an ecstatic terror of base and finer senses, before swooning into oblivion.

Presently AnsienRa awoke and, by subtle drives within, was ken to a consistent maleness, and being suitably hosted into a wandering, slack-willed human, his brain in basic order, and all else of him as required.

Well content with changeover, AnsienRa went with his body at a steady trudge down the hill. Alert as a glance, enjoying real native feelings, he gloried in all the alien variety of his twilight environment.

Within and without, he was acutely aware of every pulse of every part of him. Of the sneeze that constantly threatened the steady flow of grimy snot from his nostrils. Of the gumboil throbbing counterpulse with his heart. The chafing garment that burned in the sweat under his left armpit, the pinch of a canker stretching sorely in the crease between his buttocks. All of it was feelings – human beings' feelings, and intoxicating. His feet were points of hurt where fat, old corns punished clubbed toes, each step springing automatic winces familiar to his squinting face, twisted awry by muscles learned to pain. Different sensations assailed from center deep: waves and rolls of cramps and pressures. A rushing of blood, a thumping of heart. Subtle counterforces of containment as squeezing gurgles of gas bubbled discomfort about his entrails. The welter seeming normal stimuli, a body's sense of being well informed, but announcing that although healthy, this host was as weary as he was obstinate, as he was sharply hungry. All a flood of humanness from which AnsienRa sucked in a lust of privilege, and apprised with huge interest and continuous discovery.

Engrossed in the newness, he had followed a rude trail until it joined the end of a looseknit group straggling along. Into their minds he sought greedily and was amused and thrilled by the pervasive excitement he met, finding the people roused and gathering for common emotion and purpose.

Their fervor had woken when, two moons ago, the night skies had delivered a portent: a star! Follow for a year and it would lead to miracles. From ancient teachings, prophecy had come to pass, and folks marveled. The spectacle had ungated their minds to invasions of splendid emotional excess. And AnsienRa wallowed in engulfing swells of curiosity and awe, and faith and security and satisfaction, and even the cunning and dread which now and then tantalized their imaginations.

For a day and a night, he tagged behind one family group – man, woman, and a girl. When the sun grew stinging hot, they stopped in the meager shadow of a rocky overhang. Keeping his distance, AnsienRa had stopped too, standing droop-shouldered in the baking sunshine. And right away, from their shaded nook, the family's attention focused on him.

AnsienRa reached for their thoughts and found stirrings of sympathy in every soul, particularly the girl child. Thus, he raised soapy eyes to her.

She turned to the man. 'Papa,' she said, 'he's thirsty.'

The man looked long at AnsienRa, then at the woman, who shrugged as she fanned her face with a fold of her scarf. At which, the man took a water-bag, and shook it near his ear before trickling a bit into a bowl.

The girl picked it up, and walking gingerly with careful eyes to the bowl, stopped half the distance from AnsienRa, placed it on the ground, and slowly backed off. 'Go on, drink it. It's good,' she encouraged.

She was scarcely back to her shade before AnsienRa lurched over to the bowl, snatched it up, and slurped the water down; most of it, as over-eagerness clumsied him to spill on his chin, and neck, and chest. Although the overall relief of wetness – whether slicking the thick choke of his swallow, or soothing the singe of his skin – it touched good wherever.

From bowl, AnsienRa looked hopefully to the family, but they were busy readying to continue the trek, and paid him no mind. So he put the bowl on the burning earth and backed to a comfortable following distance, squatting in the blazing open, stolidly waiting to be their tail.

Just before nightfall, the family stopped for the night, and assembled a small tent from the bundles they carried. The woman lit a brisk bramble-fire just beyond the door-flap of their tent, and soon had a hanging pot a-bubble with the evening's meal.

AnsienRa, huddling just out reach of their fire's light, caught the pot's aromas and, teased and tortured, crept nearer and nearer to the fire. Surreptitious though he was, they fast became aware of his creeping bulk, and turned as one to him. Turned with such swift aggression, that without probing their minds, AnsienRa exactly knew their belligerence, even before the man shouted, 'Get away, you stupid idiot. Go stink somewhere else.'

And the woman threw at him the peelings of the stuff she cooked. And the girl rushed halfway at him and pelted handfuls of dirt and sand. And the man grabbed up his long staff and advanced with it mean-threatening.

Then AnsienRa turned his host's body, and clambered away trying to make sense of it.

With passing days, he discovered his idiot-host capable of withstanding extremes of physical efforts, subsisting casually, indiscriminately eating whatever, sleeping wherever tiredness took over and comfort promised enough to close his eyes. A solitary creature, to no one he made accounting, his time his own to obey but for natural calls and caprices.

As for the mind he had possessed, AnsienRa found it a-swelter from a confusion of drives in tangling contest for relevance. Briefly this or that one would usurp dominance, only to be groveling or trampled next instant. Legion concerns abused his battered reason. Events and experiences, irrelevant or major, scrambled for attention. Frights, feastings, beatings, satings, farts, chasings, fucks, killings, giggles, singings, all competed. Each weighed as every one else, the banal, the crucial, the sour, the sad, all the same.

Still, despite best efforts, the very seeker presence within did modify his base existence, although minimally, as in making him craftier at foraging, or more quickly repairing abused tissue and so being less discomforted.

Minor lifestyle improvements resulted – as with the simple strategy of quietly sitting outside the doorways of certain inns, and shaping his drooling face hungry. A tactic usually good for one meal, and by shifting from inn to inn, some days he even gorged.

Came an evening he was settled waiting at one such inn, when two well-fed men emerged generous. Chatting nearby for a moment, they noticed him, and the fatter one, with a frown, threw a coin. 'Why not pass the idiot a crumb, huh?' he observed dryly. 'Think of your afterlife.'

His bearded companion grimaced distastefully, and shrugged. 'I prefer to waste in public. In the temple.'

Nevertheless, he tossed over a half–eaten fruit, and as AnsienRa gulped and slurped the sweet pulp, the men conversed in undertones. Impatient with eavesdropping, AnsienRa entered their minds and became privy to a magnificence of dominant drives in active operation, all distantly familiar to his own body. He recognized lust, and spite, and camaraderie, each carnally spiced with a quivering anticipation.

Indignant, the heavy-set one was saying, 'He tried to stick me –'

The bearded interrupted, 'It maybe is only seeming so.'

'It was so!' the other insisted. 'He wanted to tie me to that addle-brained daughter of his.'

'No. Maybe she's touched. Gets fits. Spells, yu'know? Like her blood rising with the moon.'

'Yes, yes, whatever. But why me? Why try to trap me? I mean to say, he's my old man's friend. I mean, was. Last crop festival our families sang and ate together, yu'know what I mean? They had business together, and everything. Father couldn't believe when I broke the news on him . . .'

'I should have such a father.'

'Yeah, sure. Shouldn't we all. But it was luck, plain luck. That's what really sprung me.'

'Well, I suppose. But anyhow, yu'think it's time we should be getting over there?'

'. . . .'

'So what yu'mean? Changing your mind?'

'Nah, it's not that. I want to see. Really do. But it's a bit early, don't you think? Shouldn't we wait for the moon to rise? It's a moon thing she's got, anyhow. What yu'say?'

'Hey, you're in charge, man. Whatever you say, I'm down.'

'Don't worry, I want to see her free treat too. After all, I nearly had to pay dowry for it.'

'You mean your father nearly had, huh?'

'Same difference.'

'Guess so. So who it was that passed the news?'

'The younger one.'

'That pretty little plum?'

'Poisoned little plum, yu'mean. She's a tricky monkey, that one. Spiteful, too. And accustomed to her own way.'

'How y'mean?'

'Bet you'd never guess why she betrayed the household secret.'

'Tell me.'

'Because they, the mother, denied her a scarf, or a ribbon, or some such trinket.'

'Hmph! She doesn't look it.'

'Looks depend on the looker, brother.'

'But still you believe her?'

'Hell, yes. She wasn't composing. I could see the meanness in her eyes, shining spite and truth. She was tattling serious family secrets.'

'But still . . .'

'But nothing. It's true. I intend to show the proof.'

'Proof?'

'Yeah, sort of. Heh-heh-heh! What y'think we're about tonight? Heh-heh. You think is some wild goose chase? No, no, my brother, tonight is proof time. I know what I know 'cause last full moon, I checked.'

'You did?'

'Mmm-hmmn . . .'

'And did she?'

'Well, half and half. I didn't stay too long. Nervous, yu'know. And it was cloudy, so I didn't get to see much. But she was outside, being weird, and up to something.'

'I definitely wouldn't have shied away from that setting.'

'Come on, man. You know what'd have happened they caught me there spying? Not the scene for me, I'll say. Too much like daring the Devil.'

'Well, whatever. But time's a-passing, and our moon's coming up. You don't think we should press on now? Get in good vantage, seek a proper point of view, eh?'

And arms about each other's shoulder, they set off hearty with full-bellied laughter.

In his idiot's body, AnsienRa was trembling to an unusually powerful urge. Without exact focus, it charged about up and down his backbone and into his groin, and he well divined this yen to be same which had so moved the two fellows just gone. And compelled by the queer drive, he took after the men. Close to the ground like a shadow, employing innate seeker skills, and displaying no bit of the bumbler they would've expected, he trailed their spoor, intent on discovery.

Well concealed at the target location, AnsienRa was waiting ready when she slipped through the back door of the women's quarters and glided into the vineyard. Her sleeping shift flared and shimmered as, under the braided canopy of laden vines, she moved between moonlight and shade. Stark staring eyes, her untied hair hanging black, unkempt and plentiful gave her eerie aspect. The wild loose mane swaying sinuously, she began prancing about in strange abandon, now standing spread-legged and wiggling hips, now kneading her breasts and writhing as if in agony.

Gradually, suggestions from her intimate moves made AnsienRa come aware of the intrigue of her dance. He saw how personal and revealing her gestures were, and how uncommon an insight was the thrill he and the others were stealing.

This notion led him to search for the feelings of his fellow peepers. Not far away, he found them perched at the window of a raised room. Excited they were, and surfeited with satisfaction. And, as he sensed their pleasure at the rigid surging in their laps, he knew sympathy. His idiot's organ was engorged by this same press for fulfillment.

From commingled excitements the fatter one spoke. 'See that? See that? Huh? What did I tell you?'

'Mmm-hmmn, yeah.'

'Y'wouldn't imagine, huh? Whew! Look at that wiggle.'

'Yeah, yeah. Ssshhh . . .'

'What a pelt on her, every time she . . .'

'Ssshhh . . .'

'My-oh-my-oh-my . . .'

'Ssshhh. But you're right about that. How long she can keep that up?'

'Man, am I finding out.'

'Hey! Did y'hear that?'

'Shut up and look, man . . .'

'No, no, no. Listen. That's someone riding up the alley. Hey, when *is* this housekeep due back?'

'We have time. Don't worry. He's gone for long enough. I took good care . . . Did y'see that lowdown spread and dip?'

'Wait, man. Y'sure, huh? Huh?'

'Look. If you going to worry, let me watch. OK? There, there she goes again. Damn! On the work table. Oh-my-oh-my-oh. Look at that, huh? Didn't I tell you?'

'Whuh! Look at that skin. She's sweating readiness.'

'Mmm-hmmn, I could definitely addle with that.'

'Ssshhh . . .'

'Y'realize she's moving like that although she's practically unconscious . . .'

'Hush! Didn't you hear that? Shit! Did you latch the door? Somebody's coming up the stairs!'

'Damn! Oh damn damn damn it to hell. You're right. Quick. Quick. Close the window. Close it! Now, come, come, come here. Lay down. Right. Now shut up and hug on me. Shut up.'

'. . . !!!'

'Just pretend . . .'

'Damn!'

AnsienRa startled out as a ruckus erupted from their upper room across the roadway. A strident voice, indignant and male, was declaring threat. Another, the fatter fellow, was protesting in a wheedle when AnsienRa disengaged from their embroilment, and returned to the sinuous attraction sprawling on the work table. The better to probe the nature of her rapture, he thought to plunge into her head.

Nothing there was clear. Maybe it was his idiot's mindframe, but he could find no ties, no grips to catch on to, and relate. His masculine entity slipped incongruously over and past her essences, never stopping and touching long enough to recognize and learn. And with few clues to the nature of her impulses, AnsienRa slid out of her.

Recoiled fully into the idiot's being, he found it focused on defeating one particular frustration. Its energy – a mighty force aroused by raw instinct – was insistently directed towards one primal desire: union with the unminding female. And right then, daring and dangerous though it was, AnsienRa saw opportunity to be at the nucleus of a human matter. Saw a best-ever chance for truly finding out. There could be explaining later, but as a genuine seeker, he had to make this try.

Like a nightcloud's shade, he approached and gained where she lay in lunatic abandon. Then, slave to his and host's basest instincts,

AnsienRa surrendered to test the forbidden, and bowed to the primitive majesty of conjunction, and the charge with which Life forced generation. And shuddering at Nature's power over humans, AnsienRa lost himself to a sapping misery.

He soon left the woman, still rapt in her delusion and thrilling to its private ecstasy. Back up the craggy hills he tramped, heading as the integrating machine commanded. As he'd known he'd be. Yet he went resolute, without regret, and full-charged with seeker's bliss.

For all that he had gained, he now would have to make accounting.

Confronted by the Assembly, AnsienRa offered a pure research explanation. It was not accepted. Prime facts he so well knew, they put to him again: it was not a matter for judgment. There was strict rule against meddling. Interference muddled randomness. Tinkering adfactored entropic patterns. The contract was simple: tour without tampering.

AnsienRa suggested a final defense: 'No actual meddling occurred. Only a mind was tapped. It still would be idiot's genes.'

That met a concert of rejection: the influence of the gestalt was sufficient to organize, amplify, and direct inchoate potentials, and so create difference.

Ultimately, the wise Assembly conferred on him the established consequence of his mischance. The integrating machine – his facility for furtherance – they revoked, thus marooning him in the mind of an idiot's self-regenerating body. As onerous was their unspecified extension of his stay in semi-permanent role as observer, the Assembly's wisdom reasoned it worthwhile scholarship to monitor the extended results of his dabbling.

Thus, sentenced and forsaken, as nearly nine moons curved from circle to sickle, AnsienRa roamed that rural place, learning its primitive mores, and unraveling new perspectives of his judgment while accommodating its dictate. Until a marvel in the night sky began flaring: beacon to other seekers below, as AnsienRa knew. Reminder that it was departure time. Though not for AnsienRa. His only journey was to join the awestruck throngs attracted to the astral flare. For at its focus, he had a job to do.

A bedraggled AnsienRa paused trudging, and regarded the brilliant beacon in the heavens. He thought of how soon it'd be gone; done as lantern for alien visitors, finished as portent of unusual birth. Idiot's eyes weepy and longing, he sighed and drooled, already lonely at his surfeit of future, already feeling pointless as an echo in a hollow mind.

Then a quiet wryness slipped into his fervent gaze at the beaming from above. And, as if accepting destiny, the idiot with AnsienRa, slack in limb and will alike, set once more to tramping the gravelly hillside trail, down to the hamlet in the valley below, where ardent believers were flocking, where the moonstruck woman had journeyed to deliver her exceptional child.

another christmas

william trevor

You always looked back, she thought. You looked back at other years, other Christmas cards arriving, the children younger. There was the year Patrick had cried, disliking the holly she was decorating the living room with. There was the year Bridget had got a speck of coke in her eye on Christmas Eve and had to be taken to the hospital at Hammersmith in the middle of the night. There was the first year of their marriage, when she and Dermot were still in Waterford. And ever since they'd come to London there was the presence on Christmas Day of their landlord, Mr Joyce, a man whom they had watched becoming elderly.

She was middle-aged now, with touches of grey in her curly dark hair, a woman known for her cheerfulness, running a bit to fat. Her husband was the opposite: thin and seeming ascetic, with more than a hint of the priest in him, a good man. 'Will we get married, Norah?' he'd said one night in the Tara Ballroom in Waterford, 6 November 1953. The proposal had astonished her: it was his brother Ned, heavy and fresh-faced, a different kettle of fish altogether, whom she'd been expecting to make it.

Patiently he held a chair for her while she strung paper chains across the room, from one picture rail to another. He warned her to be careful about attaching anything to the electric light. He still held the chair while she put sprigs of holly behind the pictures. He was cautious by nature and alarmed by little things, particularly anxious in case she fell off chairs. He'd never mount a chair himself, to put up decorations or anything else: he'd be useless at it in his opinion and it was his opinion that mattered. He'd never been able to do a thing about the house, but it didn't matter because since the boys had grown up they'd attended to whatever she couldn't manage herself. You wouldn't dream of remarking on it: he was the way he was, considerate and thoughtful in what he did do, teetotal, clever, full of fondness for herself and for the family they'd reared, full of respect for her also.

'Isn't it remarkable how quick it comes round, Norah?' he said while he held the chair. 'Isn't it no time since last year?'

'No time at all.'

'Though a lot happened in the year, Norah.'

'An awful lot happened.'

Two of the pictures she decorated were scenes of Waterford: the quays and a man driving sheep past the Bank of Ireland. Her mother had given them to her, taking them down from the hall of the farm-house.

There was a picture of the Virgin and Child, and other, smaller pictures. She placed her last sprig of holly, a piece with berries on it, above the Virgin's halo.

'I'll make a cup of tea,' she said, descending from the chair and smiling at him.

'A cup of tea'd be great, Norah.'

The living room, containing three brown armchairs and a table with upright chairs around it, and a sideboard with a television set on it, was crowded by this furniture and seemed even smaller than it was because of the decorations that had been added. On the man-telpiece, above a built-in gas fire, Christmas cards were arrayed on either side of an ornate green clock.

The house was in a terrace in Fulham. It had always been too small for the family, but now that Patrick and Brendan no longer lived there things were easier. Patrick had married a girl called Pearl six months ago, almost as soon as his period of training with the Midland Bank had ended. Brendan was training in Liverpool, with a firm of computer manufacturers. The three remaining children were still at school, Bridget at the nearby convent, Cathal and Tom at the Sacred Heart Primary. When Patrick and Brendan had moved out the room they'd always shared had become Bridget's. Until then Bridget had slept in her parents' room and she'd have to return there this Christmas because Brendan would be back for three nights. Patrick and Pearl would just come for Christmas Day. They'd be going to Pearl's people, in Croydon, on Boxing Day – St Stephen's Day, as Norah and Dermot always called it, in the Irish manner.

'It'll be great, having them all,' he said. 'A family again, Norah.'

'And Pearl.'

'She's part of us now, Norah.'

'Will you have biscuits with your tea? I have a packet of Nice.'

He said he would, thanking her. He was a meter reader with North Thames Gas, a position he had held for twenty-one years, ever since he'd emigrated. In Waterford he'd worked as a clerk in the Customs, not earning very much and not much caring for the stuffy, smoke-laden office he shared with half a dozen other clerks. He had come to England because Norah had thought it was a good idea, because she'd always wanted to work in a London shop. She'd been given a job in Dickins & Jones, in the household linens department, and he'd been taken on as a meter reader, cycling from door to door, remembering the different houses and where the meters were situated in each, being agreeable to householders: all of it suited him from the start. He devoted time to thought while he rode about, and in particular to religious matters.

In her small kitchen she made the tea and carried it on a tray into the living room. She'd been late this year with the decorations. She always liked to get them up a week in advance because they set the mood, making everyone feel right for Christmas. She'd been busy with stuff for a stall Father Malley had asked her to run for his Christmas Sale. A fashion stall he'd called it, but not quite knowing what he meant she'd just asked people for any old clothes they had, jumble really. Because of the time it had taken she hadn't had a minute to see to the decorations until this afternoon, two days before Christmas Eve. But that, as it turned out, had been all for the best.

Bridget and Cathal and Tom had gone up to Putney to the pictures, Dermot didn't work on a Monday afternoon: it was convenient that they'd have an hour or two alone together because there was the matter of Mr Joyce to bring up. Not that she wanted to bring it up, but it couldn't be just left there.

'The cup that cheers,' he said, breaking a biscuit in half. Deliberately she put off raising the subject she had in mind. She watched him nibbling the biscuit and then dropping three heaped spoons of sugar into his tea and stirring it. He loved tea. The first time he'd taken her out, to the Savoy cinema in Waterford, they'd had tea afterwards in the cinema café and they'd talked about the film and about people they knew. He'd come to live in Waterford from the country, from the farm his brother had inherited, quite close to her father's farm. He reckoned he'd settled, he told her that night: Waterford wasn't sensational, but it suited him in a lot of ways. If he hadn't married her he'd still be there, working eight hours a day in the Customs and not caring for it, yet managing to get by because he had his religion to assist him.

'Did we get a card from Father Jack yet?' he inquired, referring to a distant cousin, a priest in Chicago.

'Not yet. But it's always on the late side, Father Jack's. It was February last year.'

She sipped her tea, sitting in one of the other brown armchairs, on the other side of the gas fire. It was pleasant being there alone with him in the decorated room, the green clock ticking on the mantelpiece, the Christmas cards, dusk gathering outside. She smiled and laughed, taking another biscuit while he lit a cigarette. 'Isn't this great?' she said. 'A bit of peace for ourselves?'

Solemnly he nodded.

'Peace comes dropping slow,' he said, and she knew he was quoting from some book or other. Quite often he said things she didn't understand. 'Peace and goodwill,' he added, and she understood that all right.

He tapped the ash from his cigarette into an ashtray which was kept for his use, beside the gas fire. All his movements were slow. He

was a slow thinker, even though he was clever. He arrived at a con-
clusion, having thought long and carefully; he balanced everything
in his mind. 'We must think about that, Norah,' he said that day,
twenty-two years ago, when she'd suggested that they should move
to England. A week later he'd said that if she really wanted to he'd
agree.

They talked about Bridget and Cathal and Tom. When they came
in from the cinema they'd only just have time to change their clothes
before setting out again for the Christmas party at Bridget's convent.

'It's a big day for them. Let them lie in in the morning, Norah.'

'They could lie in for ever,' she said, laughing in case there might
seem to be harshness in this recommendation. With Christmas
excitement running high, the less she heard from them the better.

'Did you get Cathal the gadgets he wanted?'

'Chemistry stuff. A set in a box.'

'You're great the way you manage, Norah.'

She denied that. She poured more tea for both of them. She said,
as casually as she could: 'Mr Joyce won't come. I'm not counting
him in for Christmas Day.'

'He hasn't failed us yet, Norah.'

'He won't come this year.' She smiled through the gloom at him.
'I think we'd best warn the children about it.'

'Where would he go if he didn't come here? Where'd he get his
dinner?'

'Lyons used to be open in the old days.'

'He'd never do that.'

'The Bulrush Café has a turkey dinner advertised. There's a lot
of people go in for that now. If you have a mother doing a job she
maybe hasn't the time for the cooking. They go out to a hotel or a
café, three or four pounds a head –'

'Mr Joyce wouldn't go to a café. No one could go into a café on
their own on Christmas Day.'

'He won't come here, dear.'

It had to be said: it was no good just pretending, laying a place for
the old man on an assumption that had no basis to it. Mr Joyce would

not come because Mr Joyce, last August, had ceased to visit them. Every Friday night he used to come, for a cup of tea and a chat, to watch the nine o'clock news with them. Every Christmas Day he'd brought carefully chosen presents for the children, and chocolates and nuts and cigarettes. He'd given Patrick and Pearl a radio as a wedding present.

'I think he'll come all right. I think maybe he hasn't been too well. God help him, it's a great age, Norah.'

'He hasn't been ill, Dermot.'

Every Friday Mr Joyce had sat there in the third of the brown armchairs, watching the television, his bald head inclined so that his good ear was closer to the screen. He was tallish, rather bent now, frail and bony, with a modest white moustache. In his time he'd been a builder, which was how he had come to own property in Fulham, a self-made man who'd never married. That evening in August he had been quite as usual. Bridget had kissed him good-night because for as long as she could remember she'd always done that when he came on Friday evenings. He'd asked Cathal how he was getting on with his afternoon paper round.

There had never been any difficulties over the house. They considered that he was fair in his dealings with them; they were his tenants and his friends. When it seemed that the Irish had bombed English people to death in Birmingham and Guildford he did not cease to arrive every Friday evening and on Christmas Day. The bombings were discussed after the news, the Tower of London bomb, the bomb in the bus, and all the others. 'Maniacs,' Mr Joyce said and nobody contradicted him.

'He would never forget the children, Norah. Not at Christmastime.'

His voice addressed her from the shadows. She felt the warmth of the gas fire reflected in her face and knew if she looked in a mirror she'd see that she was quite flushed. Dermot's face never reddened. Even though he was nervy, he never displayed emotion. On all occasions his face retained its paleness, his eyes acquired no glimmer of passion. No wife could have a better husband, yet in the matter of Mr Joyce he was so wrong it almost frightened her.

'Is it tomorrow I call in for the turkey?' he said.

She nodded, hoping he'd ask her if anything was the matter because as a rule she never just nodded in reply to a question. But he didn't say anything. He stubbed his cigarette out. He asked if there was another cup of tea in the pot.

'Dermot, would you take something round to Mr Joyce?'

'A message, is it?'

'I have a tartan tie for him.'

'Wouldn't you give it to him on the day, Norah? Like you always do.' He spoke softly, still insisting. She shook her head.

It was all her fault. If she hadn't said they should go to England, if she hadn't wanted to work in a London shop, they wouldn't be caught in the trap they'd made for themselves. Their children spoke with London accents. Patrick and Brendan worked for English firms and would make their homes in England. Patrick had married an English girl. They were Catholics and they had Irish names, yet home for them was not Waterford.

'Could you make it up with Mr Joyce, Dermot? Could you go round with the tie and say you were sorry?'

'Sorry?'

'You know what I mean.' In spite of herself her voice had acquired a trace of impatience, an edginess that was unusual in it. She did not ever speak to him like that. It was the way she occasionally spoke to the children.

'What would I say I was sorry for, Norah?'

'For what you said that night.' She smiled, calming her agitation. He lit another cigarette, the flame of the match briefly illuminating his face. Nothing had changed in his face. He said: 'I don't think Mr Joyce and I had any disagreement, Norah.'

'I know, Dermot. You didn't mean anything –'

'There was no disagreement, girl.'

There had been no disagreement, but on that evening in August something else had happened. On the nine o'clock news there had been a report of another outrage and afterwards, when Dermot had turned the television off, there'd been the familiar comment on it. He couldn't understand the mentality of people like that, Mr Joyce said yet again, killing just anyone, destroying life for no reason. Dermot had shaken his head over it, she herself had said it was uncivilized. Then Dermot had added that they mustn't of course forget what the Catholics in the North had suffered. The bombs were a crime but it didn't do to forget that the crime would not be there if generations of Catholics in the North had not been treated as animals. There'd been a silence then, a difficult kind of silence, which she'd broken herself. All that was in the past, she'd said hastily, in a rush; nothing in the past or the present or anywhere else could justify the killing of innocent people. Even so, Dermot had added, it didn't do to avoid the truth. Mr Joyce had not said anything.

'I'd say there was no need to go round with the tie, Norah. I'd say he'd make the effort on Christmas Day.'

'Of course he won't.' Her voice was raised, with more than impatience in it now. But her anger was controlled. 'Of course he won't come.'

'It's a time for goodwill, Norah. Another Christmas: to remind us.'

He spoke slowly, the words prompted by some interpretation of God's voice in answer to a prayer. She recognized that in his deliberate tone.

'It isn't just another Christmas. It's an awful kind of Christmas. It's a Christmas to be ashamed, and you're making it worse, Dermot.' Her lips were trembling in a way that was uncomfortable. If she tried to calm herself she'd become jittery instead, she might even begin to cry. Mr Joyce had been generous and tactful, she said loudly. It made no difference to Mr Joyce that they were Irish people, that their children went to school with the children of I.R.A. men. Yet his generosity and his tact had been thrown back in his face. Everyone knew that the Catholics in the North had suffered, that generations of injustice had been twisted into the shape of a cause. But you couldn't say it to an old man who had hardly been outside Fulham in his life. You couldn't say it because when you did it sounded like an excuse for murder.

'You have to state the truth, Norah. It's there to be told.'

'I never yet cared for a North of Ireland person, Catholic or Protestant. Let them fight it out and not bother us.'

'You shouldn't say that, Norah.'

'It's more of your truth for you.'

He didn't reply. There was the gleam of his face for a moment as he drew on his cigarette. In all their married life they had never had a quarrel that was in any way serious, yet she felt herself now in the presence of a seriousness that was too much for her. She had told him that whenever a new bombing took place she prayed it might be the work of the Angry Brigade, or any group that wasn't Irish. She'd told him that in shops she'd begun to feel embarrassed because of her Waterford accent. He'd said she must have courage, and she realized now that he had drawn on courage himself when he'd made the remark to Mr Joyce. He would have prayed and considered before making it. He would have seen it in the end as his Catholic duty.

'He thinks you don't condemn people being killed.' She spoke quietly even though she felt a wildness inside her. She felt she should be out on the streets, shouting in her Waterford accent, violently stating that the bombers were more despicable with every breath they drew, that hatred and death were all they deserved. She saw herself on Fulham Broadway, haranguing the passers-by, her greying hair blown in the wind, her voice more passionate than it had ever been before. But none of it was the kind of thing she could do because she was not that kind of woman. She hadn't the courage, any more than she had the courage to urge her anger to explode in their living room. For all the years of her marriage there had never been the need of such courage before: she was aware of that, but found no consolation in it.

'I think he's maybe seen it by now,' he said. 'How one thing leads to another.'

She felt insulted by the words. She willed herself the strength to shout, to pour out a torrent of fury at him, but the strength did not come. Standing up, she stumbled in the gloom and felt a piece of holly under the sole of her shoe. She turned the light on.

'I'll pray that Mr Joyce will come,' he said.

She looked at him, pale and thin, with his priestly face. For the first time since he had asked her to marry him in the Tara Ballroom she did not love him. He was cleverer than she was, yet he seemed half-blind. He was good, yet he seemed hard in his goodness, as though he'd be better without it. Up to the very last moment on Christmas Day there would be the pretence that their landlord might arrive, that God would answer a prayer because His truth had been honoured. She considered it hypocrisy, unable to help herself in that opinion.

He talked but she did not listen. He spoke of keeping faith with their own, of being a Catholic. Crime begot crime, he said, God wanted it to be known that one evil led to another. She continued to look at him while he spoke, pretending to listen but wondering instead if in twelve months' time, when another Christmas came, he would still be cycling from house to house to read gas meters. Or would people have objected, requesting a meter reader who was not Irish? An objection to a man with an Irish accent was down-to-earth and ordinary. It didn't belong in the same grand category as crime begetting crime or God wanting something to be known, or in the category of truth and conscience. In the present circumstances the objection would be understandable and fair. It seemed even right that it should be made, for it was a man with an Irish accent in whom the worst had been brought out by the troubles that had come, who was guilty of a cruelty no one would have believed him capable of. Their harmless elderly landlord might die in the course of that same year, a friendship he had valued lost, his last Christmas lonely. Grand though it might seem in one way, all of it was petty.

Once, as a girl, she might have cried, but her contented marriage had caused her to lose that habit. She cleared up the tea things, reflecting that the bombers would be pleased if they could note the victory they'd scored in a living room in Fulham. And on Christmas

Day, when a family sat down to a conventional meal, the victory would be greater. There would be crackers and chatter and excitement, the Queen and the Pope would deliver speeches. Dermot would discuss these Christmas messages with Patrick and Brendan, as he'd discussed them in the past with Mr Joyce. He would be as kind as ever. He would console Bridget and Cathal and Tom by saying that Mr Joyce hadn't been up to the journey. And whenever she looked at him she would remember the Christmases of the past. She would feel ashamed of him, and of herself.

a date with santa

mary broke freeman

There was something red lying on the snow. It was large and bulky and was sprawled on some waste ground behind the school. The children didn't see it in the dusk, as they straggled home from their nativity play. Thomas still had his crown on his head. Sarah carried the doll, still wrapped in swaddling clothes, that had stood in for baby Jesus.

Four-year-old Louis sang a carol tunelessly to himself. 'Away in a mania'. He was puzzled as he thought someone had said that Father Christmas was going to come to the party after the play, but he hadn't turned up. Louis was not surprised. Their school, an ugly flat brick of a building, didn't have a chimney, and anyway Father Christmas was meant to come at night when they were all asleep.

The teachers and the parents had made a fuss though. They'd whispered together, their faces creased with anger lines. The head mistress had told them in her extra jolly voice that Father Christmas had got held up as one of his reindeer had escaped. Some of the older children had laughed rather pityingly at her.

Penny, Louis's mother, hustled them into her house. She snapped on the light and as the children ran in to switch on the television, she said to her friend Carol, 'It's funny how Jack didn't turn up. You know how he revels in doing his good deeds.'

'I'll say he does. Maureen complained to me only last week that he seems to be on every board, committee and charity, quite forgetting that charity starts at home. She says he's never there for them.'

'Typical man, opting out of his responsibilities. You don't need to get emotionally involved with fund raising, or even visiting ill or handicapped people. Not like at home,' Penny laughed, going through to put on the kettle. 'There's enough hands on work in this house and no one lays out a red carpet for me.'

'Same here,' Carol said. 'Oh look at your cake. It's beautiful. I haven't had time, I bought mine in Marks.' She admired the white cake with its trellis icing and sugar holly leaves.

Stella, Carol's daughter, sloped in, all straggly hair and layers of garments. 'Trust Jack Leggett not turning up as Father Christmas. 'Spect he was in the pub.' At twelve years old she knew it all.

'Shh dear,' her mother warned, 'don't spoil it for the little ones. But that's most unlikely. He's usually so reliable. He must have got held up.'

'Where?' Stella didn't look convinced. 'Every year he's there, red and jolly with that awful, "Ho, ho, ho, have you been good?" Only the very smallest or thickest kids don't know it's him.'

'It's all part of the fun,' Penny said sourly. She did not like Stella much at the moment, she hoped that her Sarah would not go the same way.

'But where is he?' Stella persisted.

'I don't know,' Carol said. 'There was no answer from his home or his work.' She glanced shiftily at Penny, not wanting to voice a rumour she'd heard about Jack, in front of Stella, or they'd never hear the end of it. 'I expect we'll find out. Oh, listen, *Neighbours*.' She heard the signature tune with relief, knowing that would keep Stella occupied for a while.

Outside the village, in a secluded road banked with trees, a woman sat in a car waiting. She smoked incessantly, opening the window a crack every so often to toss away the finished butt. She looked at her watch, then the clock on the dashboard. Ten past six. He'd said he'd be here by five thirty at the latest, probably before.

'I do my Santa bit after their play, about four fifteenish. I don't stay long, don't want them to guess you know.' He'd laughed. 'Of course some of the older ones do know, or think they know. I'll come straight to our meeting place, Nina. Be waiting.' His pink face went pinker and he slipped his hand under the table to stroke her leg.

'I will, but remember your promise Jack, we can't go on meeting in such awkward places. Tell Maureen about us. Ask her for a divorce.'

'I will love, I will.' He took his hand off her leg. His face went a little tight. 'I'll tell her after Christmas.'

'I hate spending Christmas without you,' Nina said, fighting to remain dry-eyed. They sat at a small table hidden in the corner of the wine bar, trying to appear like anyone else, but they were fearful they would be seen, and stories would be sent winging back to his wife.

'I know . . . I do too. But next year.' He didn't look at her. His wife always complained that he didn't spend enough time with them.

'Surely you could have one day off your charities on Christmas Day,' she snarled, knowing his habit of visiting the old folk in the morning and the disabled veterans in the afternoon, was an excuse to get out of spending the day with her, June, their daughter and her slob of a boyfriend, Dave. Their son, Pete, hardly made contact with anyone human, so engrossed was he with his computer games.

Maureen was the only person who knew the secret of Jack's obsession with committees and charities. He longed for attention, for constant praise. He found he got it from helping others. The old, the sick, and the people who cared for them, thought he was wonderful, but they didn't have to live with him. Put up with his selfishness. The way he expected everything to be perfect in the house he was hardly ever in. Take his miniature pistols. For weeks he hardly looked at them, then suddenly he would complain they hadn't been dusted, and make a great production of cleaning them, upbraiding her all the time for being lazy.

What made it worse was the way people were always coming up to her and saying: 'What a marvellous man your husband is. He raised the money for the minibus, or revamped the day centre for the elderly.'

He did too, and it was marvellous, but not for her and the children. She'd loved him at the beginning, he was tall and dark haired, with a rakish air to him. Ironically too, she'd been attracted by his willingness to please her. Though that had only lasted until June was born.

She'd become a non-person in his life, nothing she did satisfied him. He'd never played with his children, being too busy with the handicapped and the disadvantaged. He hardly ever took her out, being at a committee meeting or a charity do, where, 'if she had any compassion', he'd said when she'd complained, she would go too. She'd tried to do her bit, but people kept telling her how marvellous Jack was, and wasn't she lucky to be married to such a kind man, until she felt so frustrated at not being able to tell them the truth, she'd stayed away. She wondered how much longer she could stand it, especially since she'd heard he'd been discussing his charity work with someone else. A younger, prettier, someone else.

'Please tell her,' Nina said to Jack again, her gazelle-like eyes pleading with him.

'I will,' he said, squeezing her hand.

Nina waited in her car in its lonely spot until a quarter to seven. It began to snow again. Big fluffy flakes, the kind that would cover the ground, and be turned, with squeaking delight by the children, into snowmen.

At last cold and despairing, Nina started for home. Why hadn't Jack come? Had Maureen found out about them? But he was going to tell her anyway and come to her. Wasn't he? Doubt, which had always jostled for a place against her love for him, swamped her. Now it was Christmas would he panic and decide to stay with Maureen and the children? She thought of them in that red brick house near the public library, the lights glowing inside, a decorated tree in the corner perhaps, with presents piled round the trunk.

To torture herself she drove past the house, but it was in darkness. The curtains drawn tight to keep their festivities inwards, for the family only. Further on she saw lighted trees in other windows and glistening decorations. A huge blow-up Father Christmas stalked across the porch of one house. She went home to her flat, a bowl of coloured glass balls and holly her only festive decoration.

She'd made a pact never to ring Jack at home, but this was the first time he had let her down without an explanation. He may ring her any moment, may have been trying while she'd waited in that dark road. She prowled round the telephone, waiting, willing it to ring. It did not. She imagined him safe in the warmth of his family. Imagined his son teasing him about dressing up as Father Christmas that afternoon. Maureen smiling proudly at him. Though perhaps she wouldn't be proud. Perhaps they were having a row about it this very moment. Jack had told her Maureen didn't understand his need to help those less fortunate than himself.

'You would never be like that,' he said warmly to her, 'you're more open hearted.'

Yet now alone, swamped with feelings of loneliness and resentment, Nina did not feel open hearted. She let self-pity take her over and wallowed in the difficulties of loving a married man.

The doorbell rang and jerked her out of her wallowing. What a fool she was being, he had come here. It was risky but he'd come. Quickly she glanced at herself in the mirror, pinching her cheeks, pushing up her hair.

'I'm coming,' she called, running to the door, fearful the neighbours would see. He'd been so particular about anyone knowing about their affair.

A small cherubic face wrapped in a woollen hat sang shrilly, 'The holly and the ivy . . .'. Four bigger children stood behind, there were adults beyond. For a moment her sinking hopes soared again thinking Jack must be there, but as she fumbled her money into their outstretched tin, she could not see him. She forced a smile and said to one of the men: 'Jack Leggett not with you this time?'

'Not tonight. I expect he's off on the razzle, old Jack.' He laughed, and collected up the children. 'Hurry now, we've one more stop before the snow gets too bad. Happy Christmas Nina, it looks like being a white one this year.'

'Happy Christmas,' she echoed, though her heart was sore.

An hour later she telephoned Jack, at home. He'd promised to tell Maureen after Christmas, that was in two days time so if she jumped the gun a bit, it was just too bad. There was no answer.

The next day the snow had stopped falling. The sky was clear blue. The children swarmed from their houses in excitement, dragging sledges, trays, even dustbin liners to hurtle down the hill behind the church. They built snowmen, had snowball fights. Their mothers thankful for a few hours quiet to finish their preparations.

Nina, who would be spending Christmas Day with her brother and his large family, had no preparations to make. She went to look for Jack.

She saw Penny sorting out a snowball fight, extracting snow from a screaming Louis's neck. When he'd calmed down, she said: 'How was the play?'

'Very noisy this year. They had a percussion band, the cymbals kept going off at the most unlikely places.'

'And the party afterwards?'

Penny, hoping to get on doing up the presents while the children were out, was halfway to her door. 'It was fine.'

'And Jack did his Father Christmas well?'

Penny turned round and scrutinized her. She knew the rumours as well as the next person. Nina worked in the administration at the local hospital, Jack had often worked alongside her on one of his many projects.

'No, as a matter of fact he didn't,' she said darkly. The snow and Christmas had worked the children up to a frenzy, she was exhausted and grumpy.

'What do you mean?' Nina looked anxious.

'He didn't turn up. All the children were excited, looking forward to it, and he didn't show up,' Penny said sharply. She went inside and shut her door firmly. She and Carol had assumed he'd been waylaid with Nina. In fact they'd had quite a giggle over the thought of Jack making love to Nina while dressed up as Father Christmas.

Nina stood stock still staring at the closed door with its holly wreath hanging at an angle on it. A snowball whizzed passed her landing at her feet, another hit Thomas who screamed, running over to Louis who'd thrown it with such precision, yelling at him.

'You cheated, I wasn't ready.' He was bundling more snow in his hand as he ran.

'I wasn't. I'll tell if you hit me again. Then Father Christmas won't come.' Louis sang and danced away, keeping his eye on the door to rush for his mother should Thomas get too rough.

'Baby! Baby! He's dead. Father Christmas is dead,' Thomas said.

Louis stopped, his lower lip quivered, his eyes large. 'He's not,' he said unconvincingly.

''Course he is. He couldn't live for hundreds and hundreds of years. He's older than Grandpa and he's dead,' Thomas said with satisfaction.

'He's not, he's not.' Louis began to run to his mother, then a thought struck him and he stopped, bumping into Nina. 'Jesus isn't dead.' He cowered slightly, squinting up at Nina in case she shouted at him. She didn't seem to notice him and walked away up the road.

She went to Jack's house. Walked right up to the door and rang the bell. She barely thought of what she would say, but she was determined to find Jack and ask him why he hadn't turned up. There was no answer. She rang again, knocked loudly on the tarnished knocker, anger mounting in her. Had he run out on her? Had the whole Christmas thing made him decide it was wiser to stay with his wife?

A woman from across the road called to her. 'You won't get an answer, they've gone.'

'What?' Nina went over to her, staring stupidly at her. 'Gone? Gone where?'

'On a cruise. Went the day before yesterday.' There was a gleam of importance in the woman's eyes as she gave this news.

'All of them?' Nina's mouth was dry.

'Well, not the boyfriend.'

'But . . . Jack?' She hardly dared ask.

'Of course.' The woman gave her a suspicious look. 'He was joining them in London. He had a meeting, but doesn't he always?'

'You're sure?' Nina felt she would faint.

'Of course I'm sure.' The woman looked indignant. 'I saw them go, they took an awful lot of luggage too. I told Maureen she'd sink the boat.'

Nina dragged herself away, hardly knowing where she was going. Only last month she'd begged Jack to take her away for a weekend before Christmas, just a weekend, but he'd said he couldn't. No wonder, he was keeping his money for this cruise. He'd never breathed a word. She couldn't believe he'd betrayed her so.

Penny and Carol slumped in front of the fire, deflated, exhausted after the trauma of Christmas.

'Only one more day before they go back to school,' Penny said thankfully. 'It seems to have gone on for ever, and I seem to have seen no one but the family.'

'I know. Oh, you'll never guess,' Carol straightened up flushed with her news, 'you know why Jack never turned up as Father Christmas? They went on a cruise.'

'A cruise?' Penny sat up too.

'Yes. They all packed off the day of the play.' Carol looked pleased with the effect her story was having.

'They can't have done. I mean if they were going on one, Maureen would never have stopped going on about it. The whole place would have known every detail of where they were stopping, what they were seeing. Where did you hear that?'

'Kate Crow who lives opposite. She says a woman, I think it must have been Nina, was knocking, almost pounding, she said, on their door. So she didn't know either.'

'But why didn't they tell us? Why didn't Jack say he couldn't do his Father Christmas bit, as he was going away?' Penny didn't look convinced.

Carol shrugged. 'I would say he didn't want Nina to know. Wanted to escape from her. But how he managed to make Maureen keep from telling everyone goodness knows.' She laughed.

There was a scream from the garden, running feet, 'Mum . . . Mum, Thomas hit me.'

Penny sighed. 'Roll on school,' she said.

The school caretaker, pottering round to get things ready for the children, found something large and bulky dressed in red sprawled under the snow on the waste ground behind the school.

zizi

mandla langa

I am running along this beach, which has been reclaimed. The signs, once empowered to prescribe swathes of landscape for particular communities, are now down. The vegetation thrives and there is everywhere the taste of salt in the air. The muddy banks of the river which flows into the sea support bulrushes and haulms of sedge. Out of the vast, restless sea comes a blast of spume which gives an effect of something big and ineffable insinuating itself into lives of ordinary people. The aquamarine surface of the sea shimmers, changes and assumes the colours of the sun; spangled bubbles summon the memory of precious stones.

There is something unreal about this scene which suggests that one is inside a many-layered dream, which peels off, like an onion, and introduces the dreamer to another experience. Armed with this knowledge that I might wake up to another illusion, I am not fooled by appearances. What is real is real. But I am also familiar with wet dreams of fulfilment in a hungry world.

This realization that we operate without trust and expect life to be hard and happiness to be recalled only in misery, causes me to wonder what will finally become of us. We are like orphans bereft of the head of the household, where mirrors and all the artefacts of remembrance get covered by a shroud which shields the profaned life from the nakedness of our eyes.

The sea voices its neutrality, but the waves crashing against the rocks, the iridescent spray, fail to appease my personal anger. I imagine that the rage speaks to the elements. The rollers, it seems, are not so much enraged as surprised that something so sacred and dear could have been blasphemed.

There are few people left who will remember what this stretch of land and water once meant to us. Most of my former friends and playmates are gone. Some of those who remained retreated into an inner world whose silence transcends the grave. They are there, but they are also not there. To try and prise them out of torpor, to wake the sleepwalker in them, is an act more desperate than indulgence in fantasies. Because I am one of them, and I find myself going through the motions of living, I have arrogated the right to tell my story, which is also their story.

But, an idea hits me. No, this is Zizi's story, and you know Zizi. He is the thing that bursts inside you, at the same time making you feel whole, as if you had a heart. Something pulses in that corner of a man's chest where such activity throbs. And you feel it won't stop, even if Zizi is pushing you to it, until you explain who he was, is, this boy, Zizi, who died in the docks.

As I run, feeling the sand subsiding beneath my toes, I marvel at the arrogance of it all. I believe I am a rational man, but, then, which ghost is not given to a little self-delusion?

Zizi is unhelpful when it comes to unravelling the narrative; he knows that no one can imagine what we went through. And he can play the fool because he is dead, and death has been known to bring about great irresponsibility: people cannot touch you. Which is strange in some way, because, of the group, Zizi was the most considerate. He would say to you, '*Thuthuka* – bless you!' when you sneezed (or even when you coughed). And he would help old women with their shopping baskets from the Indian Market on Victoria Street on Saturday mornings. And they would not even say to him: 'Go away, you little scamp!' as they were wont to react to us.

He was that kind of boy, very dependable. It possibly came from the fact that his one leg was shorter than the other, I cannot remember which, and he walked with a pronounced limp. We would never make fun of him, because Zizi had the strongest arms south of the

Equator and could wrestle the most well-built of us to the ground. I have been hit in my days, even by big policemen, but nothing beats the morning when Zizi slapped me across the face for calling him a fool, the ringing in the ears, the stars that swam and the tears that sprang into my eyes.

It was Siza who suggested it, that since we were on summer holidays, and we were beginning to take an interest in girls, who were certainly noticing the rags we wore, we should get holiday jobs. The fashion in the township of KwaMashu consisted of Sta-Press trousers or Levi's jeans, Converse sneakers, Viyella button-down shirts; sometimes a black wind-breaker with a ribbed collar above a BVD T-shirt. No imitations.

'There's no work, Siza,' someone complained, 'not in Durban.'

'Yes,' I supplied. 'Our fathers trudge the pavements seeking work . . .'

'Don't tell us about your father.' It was Zizi. 'He's a priest. The only trudging he does is from Genesis to Malachi.'

'Still . . .'

Siza snapped: 'Still nothing. Just look at us.' He sounded angry. 'Cast-offs from brothers, uncles. No self-respecting scarecrow would be seen dead in these –' he judged himself, '– rags.' For a moment, it was as if he wanted to cry. But, being fourteen, it wouldn't have been the right thing to do.

I was also fourteen. Changes were happening in my head; some, in that distant, confused moment, in my body. When this happened to you, you realized that the pillars you had heard so much about which, maybe, Samson shook, are still there, intact, gearing up to demonstrate, with a vengeance, that your old man was talking shit. Something curdles up in you, love, and you remember that you are your father's son.

Which was all fine. These noble notions. Who was Zizi's father?

I remember him as someone I could have possibly worked at liking. Trim, dapper; Arrow shirts. He wore shoes that gleamed, and it was clear that this was patent leather, maybe Italian. Moustache flecked with assigned grey. He had a car, a Valiant, which he used to rev for a while before driving off. Zizi: 'He's OK, my dad. Full of things.' Pause, speculative. His eyes did not need to talk. 'Ma's sleeping. Feel I have to ask you to be here when we do the asking. You mind?'

'No. Fine with me.'

'Fix you sommin'? Tea? Coffee?' Then Zizi cursed. 'Know you hate all that. Coke? Seven-Up?'

'Seven-Up.'

My township, KwaMashu – which very few people want to claim – is there. I suspect that in those hidden corners in which I stuck my broad nose – and people were offended – something waited with a bated breath. Mine was a township of copses and darkness. Looking at the areas abutting the stations of KwaMashu and Tembalihle: is that not where we grew up and plotted about robbing the post office and Sithole's supermarket? An area so full of humankind where you hear the sound of sizzling fat-cakes, juicy sausages on a griddle or jive to the latest tune today, baby, cause tomorrow it would be gone.

As a preacher's son, whatever I said, I was a victim of my parentage. I would come up with the most daring idea for mischief, but the fellows would shake their heads and roll their eyes and make me feel useless. My clothes were cast-offs from the congregations. I was an emotional case whose survival was determined by the prosperity of the believers and their weekly tithes. A pariah. This was unbearable.

My father did not come from South Africa. He had traversed the length and breadth of the northern Transvaal. Messina. Bushbuckridge. There is a story connecting him to countenancing not only the lions but thunder. He was black, yes, but he spoke Zulu with an accent, which was not lost on my friends. My mother, understanding my bewilderment, did not fight me. She used the family. There were always, in the context of our holy, pentecostal church, rituals to redeem the sinner and bring him to the altar of the alabaster Christ.

I did not hear her, Zizi's mother, until she was upon us, speaking from behind me, in that voice. 'So,' she said, 'you elected to feed yourself, huh? Zizi?'

This is where I escape, I thought. Tongue stinging with the fizz of Seven-Up, I turned from the kitchen stool to look at her. An ordinary mother in a faded pink housecoat. Possibly sensing my intention, she brought her elbow down with a thump on the table and looked at me. 'This what you being taught at home,' she asked. 'Just coming in and having a right royal time?'

'Ma –?'

'Don't you Ma me, Zizi. This is stupid.' Her mouth trembled. She was the most beautiful, desirable woman I had ever seen, really. Skin like black velvet, I wanted to touch her. I realized, at that exact moment, why our country would never survive as long as it continued to lie to itself.

'Where would you find work?' She was talking to her son but I had a feeling she was addressing me. Being hopelessly in love with her, I imagined all sorts of things. But I decided to keep my mouth shut.

'The docks, Ma,' Zizi said. 'Boys are being taken on as casual labour.'

She made a sucking sound with her teeth. 'And you think you'll survive there?' She barked out once, a harsh laugh which sounded like a sob. The sunlight washed the kitchen table and bounced against her face. She caught me looking at her and something like a cold flame flickered in her eyes, once, twice, and disappeared. I still wonder what she thought of me. She probably divined that I was shy; maybe she concluded that I was somewhat retarded.

I was sure she had sensed me watching her on the weekly occasion when she hung the washing on the line, tossing socks and underwear like a netball player, the fabrics arcing in the piercing morning air to land on the clothes line, she was that good. Like all mothers, she had a great capacity to instil guilt in a boy. 'Does your mom and dad know about this?' This time she was talking to me.

'Yes,' I lied. Growing up in the theatre of the church creates the most accomplished liars. My mother and father would have had a seizure apiece if they knew what we were planning. I had had my fair share of beatings by my father when I forgot to water the plants or light the paraffin lamps at dusk. My response to all this was that I had to take it like a man; I felt that I deserved the punishment. What I feared most was to be thrashed by my mother. Anyone who knows the intimate pain of carrying you for nine months – and the wrenching terror of childbirth – knows something about her issue's threshold of pain, how to turn on the screws and elicit the appropriate scream. Mothers are bad news. Which is why the teachers, when faced with a rebellious student, always used this threat: 'I will call your mother to the school.' This had an effect of bringing about a lasting peace.

Zizi's mother didn't believe me, I know this. But, when she shook her head and looked at the weeds that were rubbing their backs against her fresh maize stalks, she relented and agreed that Zizi should come with me. It could have been for any number of reasons. The streets were out there baring their teeth and flexing their muscles, ready to claim any boy. The streets swaggered in threes or fours and loitered around the *stoeps* of shops, blowing fogs of sickly sweet smelling Durban Poison. They pursed their lips and whistled at young women and cursed old men and flashed the blade at the slightest provocation. In a small way, then, I think, Zizi's mother must have been grateful that her son was not regarded as an oddity, that he was part of the royal fellowship of something nearest to wholesome boyhood. If she only but knew.

It was just our luck that on our first day out it was raining as if the heavens had gone crazy. Durban had always been a wet city; but on this occasion, the impression I got was that the rain was coming down not so much as a climatic necessity: it had assumed a life of its own, the same way musical notes sometimes come out of the brass bell of a trumpet to enjoy their own selves. The nights in Durban were like that, too; nights that proclaimed their own nocturnal nature, something which confounded the brightest torches.

On this wet Monday morning, we queued out at the bus rank. By the time we were inside, we were soaked to the skin. The interior of the bus was overwhelmed by Jackson's cigar smoke. He was a thin Malawian, as black as tar. It seemed that he smoked the evil smelling cigars to irritate the women who were on their way to the madams' kitchens. They were discouraged from opening the windows because the cold air which carried icy raindrops was more unbearable than Jackson's fumigation.

'These MaNyasa,' the women would hiss, 'coming here with their strange ways!' MaNyasa was a derogatory term used for people who came from Malawi. If Jackson heard this, he did not let on. He puffed on, his ebony face as serene as a river. We certainly couldn't say anything to him because Jackson was our key to the shipyard construction company called Forrest Guniting.

The bus roared on, picking up passengers on every stop until it was so packed that breathing was difficult; an aunty dared slide the window open to let in respirable air. We passed the brace of industrial buildings near The Point; a few feet to the left rose the grim greyness of The Point prison, its walls as sturdy as a fortress. We followed Jackson out two stops further up. He led us to a clearing where a barracks-style prefabricated building stood forlornly. He knocked on the door, took off his hat and went in.

'What do you think will happen?' I asked.

'We'll see,' Siza said. 'Just don't get nervous. Jackson knows what he's doing.'

'Water is seeping in through my shoes,' I complained.

'Bugger the water,' Siza said. He was nervous despite the show of bravado.

A few minutes later, Jackson came out followed by two white men in hard hats. One was big with a beer belly; his companion was as thin as a rake, but there was something about them, the way they regarded each other, which made them seem like brothers. The thin one cleared his throat. My father always cleared his throat before making a long speech.

'My boys,' he said, 'I don't know what Jackson has been telling you. Be that as it may, we are here to work. I'm taking you to the docks, we are going to sweat there, make no mistake. You'll be paid hourly. If you work hard, we'll get along fine. If you don't, you'll soon know why men have given me a certain nickname.'

A white van with the company name stencilled on the side panels pulled up. We were waved into the back. Jackson sat in the cab with the thin white man and an African driver in blue denim overalls. We could see traffic along Congella, the brownstone building of the Electricity Supply Commission, the smoke billowing from the twin towers of the Hullets sugar company. To the right, people were already queuing up to enter the King Edward VIII hospital. We were headed for Mobeni.

'What is his nickname?' I asked.

'People call him *Mlom'wengwenya* – the mouth of the crocodile.' Zizi seemed to know everything.

'I wonder why he's got a name like that.'

'You'll have enough time to find out,' Siza said. 'In the mean time why don't you all shut up, maybe we can hear what they're cooking up in front.'

We pricked up our ears but could hear little above the roar of the traffic and the bone-rattling bumps as the wheels hit the potholes. Soon enough we were passing through Clairwood, the gum-trees and wattles paving the road, bougainvillaea and jasmine drooping in the rain. Indian and Coloured people milled about, some ducking the downpour, throwing themselves under bus shelters. Some schoolchildren in uniform emerged from the houses, satchels knocking against young, bobby-soxed legs and Bata shoes. The settlements were waking up.

We reached the industrial site at 6.45 a.m. Men were already readying themselves for work, stripping off their ragged street clothes to put on even more ragged overalls. Sandblasting equipment began to whir; then, a powerfully built man whose torso glistened with perspiration and rain started the siren. It was one of the loudest sounds I had ever heard.

We were parcelled off to the dry dock where we climbed down the long steel ladder riveted to the wall. Down below was sludge which we were required to shovel into a big bucket. This was in turn winched up and out and emptied. Then it was lowered down again and the cycle began. Crocodile's corpulent friend called us out around eleven o'clock. We were then assigned to the shipyard detail where we were installed on suspended planks where we applied carmine industrial coating on ship plates. The water, some thirty feet below, was dirty; it swirled with rotting timber and the detritus of industry. High above us, some other casual labourers were chipping paint off the deck using hammers, the din deafening. Someone had brought a radio; the FM station was loud with Christmas carols; this was accompanied by the voice of the announcer telling us about the goodness of our leaders during whose benevolent watch we were nearing the commemoration of Christ's birthday.

The siren signalling lunch sounded and we made our way to the steady ground at the industrial site. The three of us crept under a trailer and munched our peanut-butter sandwiches and washed them down with tepid tea from Zizi's flask. I was already dog tired; my two friends weren't faring any better. I looked out at the sea which was grey and you couldn't see where it ended and the sky started. A lone liner cruised slowly across the water; its sight brought about a yearning that was almost insupportable. I wished we had been born elsewhere under different circumstances, where we wouldn't have to work so hard just to buy Christmas clothes. I wished that my father were rich and owned an Oldsmobile in which he would take us to the beach on Sundays. Siza, who had been lying on his back staring at the trailer's chassis, suddenly turned and rested on his elbows.

'What in hell are we doing here?' he asked.

'It was all your idea,' I said. 'Wasn't it?'

'Stop this bickering,' Zizi said. Then he seemed to consider. 'I hear say that they'll give us a bit extra come Christmas week.'

'Says who?' I asked.

'Jackson. He got it from Crocodile.'

'I'll be damned if I'm setting foot here tomorrow,' Siza swore. 'What kind of place is this? You know that guy who starts the siren? He's deaf and dumb. That explains why he works like a madman.'

'Don't know about you fellows,' Zizi says, 'but I have to come back. Again and again.'

This made Siza and me a little ashamed because we were bigger and healthier than Zizi. Here he was now, making us seem like whingeing ninnies. I thought of challenging Siza on his statement which suggested that deaf and dumb people were mules. But before I could advance an argument, the siren screamed once, twice; the lunch period was over and we were back to our assigned posts.

The day passed and we were handed our pay. We took the bus home after establishing that we would come back the next day. Zizi had won. We all slept all the way in the bus and were woken up by Jackson near our stop. 'See you tigers tomorrow.' He disappeared into a shebeen.

We dragged ourselves to the bus stop the following morning, and the day after, for one week. The routine was beginning to make sense. We could even play tricks on Jackson and Crocodile. Just when everything was becoming familiar, we were transferred to cleaning the ship's engine.

Meanwhile, life of exertion becomes enjoyable; the air thickens and I feel the strain in my calves as the water and sand pull at my feet. People pass, some are running, like me, but most of them content themselves with walking and enjoying the morning on the seaside. Someone passes, his radio or what the kids nowadays call the boombox blasts loud soul music, Arthur Conley, I think. There is something sorrowful and optimistic about the singer's voice. It is the voice of someone familiar with pain. For me it is a balm. I run on. And as I follow the footprints of an earlier walker, I see the celebrants baptizing the believers in the water; a knot of robed people sing and beat on drums. There is a slower tempo beneath the spiritual, and beneath it the moaning of a woman, someone in the throes of a nameless peril and I remember Zizi when he screamed.

The engine room was unlike several ones I had seen in factories where I delivered messages to some members of my father's church.

The boilers were larger but cleaner here; the flames behind glass panels convinced me that they were not using coal for fuel. Since the ship was stationary, the furnaces and boilers were merely for providing heating for the cabins and perhaps hot water for the showers used by the Belgian crew on the upper decks.

We were issued with miners' hats strapped with little torches on the front, well-worn gloves and buckets in which swirled a corrosive detergent. Our task was simply to follow a narrow chamber and scoop the grease from the machinery. The heat inside was intense and I could actually feel heat rash covering the exposed areas of my body. It was filthy work and the odour of the detergent, which must have been highly flammable, made it feel dangerous.

Since Zizi was slighter in build, he was required to lead us. We crawled on our bellies and slid through vertical and horizontal channels, shovelling the goo into the buckets with our hands. My torch went out and I was plunged into a carbon darkness, something deeper than the darkness experienced when you shut your eyes tight at night. I followed what I thought was the route which Zizi had taken. I could not, also, hear Siza, who was supposed to be behind me. Terror clawed at me. I whispered, 'Zizi?' My voice bounced back at me. I removed the gloves and tried to feel my way about, and my hand capsized the bucket. The liquid splashed against the floor and into my eyes. I screamed once as my eyes burnt; the scream, even when I had stopped, continued ringing, a sound that was louder than the lunchtime siren. Zizi was screaming at the top of his voice.

I do not know to this day how I made my way out. But I do remember sitting on the deck, retching, while Siza thumped my shoulders asking what had happened. Where was Zizi? In that almost tranquil moment, there was an urgent throbbing in my temples as if my head would burst open like an over-ripe watermelon. A man in a captain's uniform was gesturing animatedly as he talked to Crocodile, the latter seeming to have lost his characteristic swagger. A siren sounded, but this time it was not jarring; it carried a certain sad and valedictory tone which accentuated the stillness of the afternoon. Some birds soared above us and left a silver after-image of themselves as they dived into the water.

After what seemed like an eternity, Siza came up from behind and stroked my cheek with a greasy hand. I turned to look up at him and it was in his face that I read what had happened. 'He's dead, isn't he?' I asked.

'Yes,' Siza said. 'He was trapped in the propeller shaft and they couldn't haul him out.' There was a wildness about his movements which contrasted strangely with the serenity in his eyes. I held his gaze before my eyes were drawn to the dull gleam of the captain's polished shoe leather. Set alongside these were Crocodile's scuffed *veldskoene*. The two men were still arguing some point heatedly when I stood up and lunged at Crocodile, beating him about the face, screaming until hands pulled me back and pinioned me against the railing.

We buried Zizi on Christmas Eve on the grounds of the new cemetery in KwaMashu. Some children from our class attended, their faces transformed by their inability to comprehend what had happened. Zizi's mother and father stood over the mound, bonded by the tragedy but seeming more isolated from each other than ever before. When Zizi's mother raised her face to look at the sun, I understood the terrible beauty of bereavement.

I heard later that Forrest Guniting paid vast sums of money. Zizi's parents separated with the mother settling somewhere else, in the city. Zizi's father drifted from one woman to another; he changed cars, but he had lost his township hipster strut. Much later, he hit the bottle with a vengeance and nearly got killed in a car crash. Eventually, he also moved from KwaMashu and I heard that he was in Clermont Township running taxis.

Siza and I found that we had nothing in common. Our friend's death had also killed the tenuous link between us. He left school and worked as a bus conductor; on the rare occasion I bumped into him, he looked sadder and heavier and sounded infinitely coarser. I knew that he would in time join some Holy Roller sect and scale even higher reaches of self-delusion.

It was when we were writing our Matriculation exams that I was visited by Zizi. I remember that I was struggling with a biology paper trying to figure out how to label a cross-section of the eye. Zizi pulled up a chair and sat down beside me. He had put on weight in death and his face glowed as if he were using skin lightening creams. He smiled as he handed me a piece of paper where the drawing was clearly labelled. I must have been so surprised that I cried out. The invigilator gave me a disapproving look and threatened to throw me out. 'Don't panic,' Zizi whispered. 'Here,' he said sliding a white envelope under my question papers. 'This is for Ma. The address is written outside. Tell her I'm OK.' He looked at me and I saw that his eyes were full of unexpressed desires. When I next looked he was gone.

That afternoon I took a bus to Sycamore Road in town. I found the address without difficulty. Zizi's mother was there, in a maid's pink uniform. She looked at me with neither welcome nor hostility, just a bland acceptance of something inevitable. She took the envelope and thanked me politely. When I started to ask her a question, she placed a forefinger against my lips. I caught the smell of Lifebuoy soap and fresh linen. Then she closed the door firmly against my face.

I am tired now but I still punish myself. I do a U-turn and head back to where I started. The baptism is still going on. As I run I remember all the people, all the faces we confronted in our attempts to confront ourselves. There were those children with whom I left in 1976 after the slaughter in Soweto. Running on this beach I recall how we resolved to return and claim what was ours. In all that time in unfamiliar lands where I sought a salve in the arms of strangers, I hankered for a possibility to unravel the mystery of Zizi's death and reappearance. I asked myself many questions, whether I had imagined it all, if this had not been conjured up by a feverish mind.

I see the woman, freshly emerged from the water, holding on to the arms of the preacher. Zizi's mother looks older and more frail. Dressed in white robes she seems more wraith-like than her undead son. She raises her eyes possibly to look at the sky for signs of her living god and they meet mine. It is eyes that have watched so many rise, so many stagger and go under. They have borne witness to everything: from the acres in the plantations to the miles of scrubbed kitchen floors; the hundreds of thousands of little sons and daughters of the masters of the land understanding love as they nestle in the bosoms of despised mamas. They will be there, these eyes, to remind us of our folly when we stagger, here, on the horizon, now in this stammering season and they will teach us the innocence of violence and the value of miracles.

I do not say anything. The sand beckons, and the believers continue their ceremony of endurance.

minna's stuffing

michele hanson

Minna had always been thrilled by the price of turkey. She still is. It is now cheaper than anything – cheaper than beef, than lamb, even cheaper than chicken. Starting with this outstanding bargain gives her a boost, a determination to create the dish of the year with this, the cheapest of ingredients. So she throws herself into her work, creating a stuffing of great magnificence. Her husband Maurice has always been keen on turkey.

This is not her festival – Christmas. She doesn't believe in Jesus. As a Jew, she is still waiting for the Messiah, but she has always gone for the presents, for her daughter Selina. Not just a stocking full, but a pillowcase of them, and a large, stuffed turkey.

Minna has never admired Christians. She supplied Selina with bits of information about them as Selina grew up. Christians often ate spam and fish paste and cooked in lard. They did not wash daily and consequently did not always have clean bottoms. Royalty was exempt from this criticism, but even the English aristocracy were suspect. Only the Jews ate and washed properly. This is what Minna believed.

Of course she recognized the odd exception. The Robertson family round the corner were Christian but generous. They ate Bisto gravy, but Selina was given huge meals when she stayed there and the family members were all scrupulously clean. They kept up these standards effortlessly, as though it were natural to them. They didn't even have to mention such things. Food, bowels and excrement were not an important feature of their daily lives.

Minna's sister Zelda, on the other hand, paid constant attention to her bowels. She had to. She often described her struggle to Minna. In order to go out in the morning, she began preparations the day before. She poured boiling water over four large prunes first thing, soaked them all day and ate them last thing at night. Then she could go to the lavatory successfully the next morning, then she could wash her bottom, then she could go out. Otherwise she was a prisoner in her own house. She would even have to cancel the hairdresser. She felt, as Minna did, that a woman's bottom should never smell and should only be touched through a flannel.

But she never forgot it was there. Neither did Minna. They never forgot it for a minute. The Christians did, especially at Christmas. Here they were, celebrating a birth resulting from an immaculate conception. Once again they had ruled out bodily functions. So it was clear to Zelda and Minna that the Jews were different. They were realists. Minna did not count Jesus as one of them. He was an impostor. She wasn't impressed by his origins or miracles or socialist principles. And she was particularly averse to the sight of him hanging up. Her daughter Selina had inherited this aversion, so the only bits of practice they took to at home were the presents and the turkey.

As a child Selina had always been excited by Christmas. It was an attractive festival: sparkling trees, the sack of presents, holidays, lovely music. They had lovely music at her school, a carol service practised to perfection. Jews were not allowed to join in. As a special treat Jews were allowed to watch the final rehearsal from the gallery. It ran all round three sides of the hall, this gallery, but at the top end, above the platform where the headmistress stood, the wall was decorated by a replica piece of Parthenon Frieze.

Selina would imagine herself saving the school from a stampeding herd of muscular, white Parthenon horses. Alone, she would bring them to a skidding, snorting halt on the school lawn, just before they trampled the infants and demolished the side of the

building. There she would be, a slight figure in grey shorts and
Aertex shirt, holding the sweating herd by a handful of reins. The
whole school would suddenly recognize her dedication to it and her
magical way with horses.

At the carol rehearsal, from her place in the gallery, Selina could
look down upon the neat rows of girls below, sitting on the parquet
floor with their legs crossed, hands on their knees, or standing in
perfect lines and singing beautifully. Then here and there she would
see a slight scuffle and sudden space as the odd girl fainted and was
carried away.

She was very keen to join in with this Christmas singing. Just this,
not the everyday hymn singing. Jews missed daily assembly as well.
They were allowed, together with the Catholics, to file into the hall
at the end of prayers and listen to the notices. All through prayers
they sat in a classroom next to the hall doing whatever homework
they hadn't yet done, and Naomi Schlesinger was always naughty.
She climbed on desks, talked and laughed and was rude to prefects,
but she was ever so clever, and perhaps because of her and her
friends, the Jews were assumed to be collectively naughty.

They were also fortunate. They had that extra half-hour every
day during prayers in which to finish their homework. Sometimes,
when Naomi Schlesinger was quiet, Selina could hear the hymns
coming from the hall. She rather liked *For Those In Peril On The Sea*,
but *There Is A Green Hill Far Away* upset her, particularly the
discord on 'crucified'. It made her feel chilly and rather sick. On that
chord she felt that there was perhaps something sinister about the
Christian religion. But the carols were different. They were not
about the bleeding, semi-naked man hanging up and looking mal-
nourished. For Christmas you only had stars, trees, kings, holly and
little bits of Latin. If you wanted to, you could even exclude Jesus
altogether, rather as they do now in Inner London ethnically mixed
primary schools.

Year after year Selina had listened to the girls singing carols, and
eventually, when she was fourteen, there came a year when she
wanted more than ever to join in. She wanted very much not to be

in the homework classroom or the gallery, but to be out there in the hall making that beautiful noise. She was absolutely sure, that year, that God existed. It was Him towards whom her singing would be directed. She felt that in her soul she could bypass Jesus. She nagged and nagged until Minna wrote to Headmistress and asked if she might join in.

Minna received a very crushing reply. 'It is all or nothing,' wrote Headmistress strictly. It was babies and stars *and* wounds and thorns, or nothing. Which was only fair really, but Minna was terribly embarrassed by it. For years she reminded everyone of this rejection whenever she thought of it. Any mention of education, injustice or an unreasonable demand could easily bring it to mind: 'Do you remember, you made me ask her and she wrote and said . . .'

To Minna, this ultimatum from Headmistress was a brutal reminder that the Christians never gave the Jews anything for nothing. She should never have asked. Whenever possible, Maurice had always stressed the independence of the Jews. Who helped them when they first came to this country? Nobody. They helped them-selves. The Jewish Board of Deputies looked after them, not the Social Security. Not the Christians. Maurice himself strongly resembled Jesus, being suntanned, bearded and exceptionally thin. Minna would remind him of this when he was out of favour. It was no compliment.

After Headmistress, Minna stuck to the stuffing. It was, in fact, an Irish recipe, given to Minna by an Irish cook of immense skill and wisdom, but no one knew that.

Minna made the stuffing from chestnuts, mushrooms and lemons. The chestnuts had to be boiled and then peeled by hand, lots of them. This is a gruelling task, picking away at chestnut skins, even when they have been blanched. Then it all has to be mixed up and stuffed in and the turkey sewn up.

But Minna continued to do it, year after year, and every year it was perfect. Selina, all through her childhood and youth, ate it annu-ally. The sack of presents stopped but the stuffing continued, retain-ing its high standard however dismal the Christmas. And as Selina grew older and remained childless, the Christmases grew more desolate. At last Selina provided Minna with a granddaughter, Sophie, who, even when small, loved turkey. As an infant she rejected the stuffing, but still Minna produced it, slaving away every Christmas, till now, in her eighties, the heat, the time and the effort are almost too much for her.

The weight of the turkey in its roasting pan is enormous. She cannot turn it unaided. It is a difficult and dangerous task. Boiling fat surrounds the turkey, increasing the risk.

Together Minna and Maurice open the oven door and try to carry out the hot and spluttering turkey. Suppose one of them was to fall? Selina tries to help them. They resent her interference but she insists on performing this hazardous part of the turkey cooking. Minna is frightened all the same. Because to her Selina, although aged fifty, is still a child – an incompetent, unable to safely carry a pan of hot fat. She may, as she turns the turkey over, allow it to flop back into the roasting pan, splashing fat and injuring herself, the granddaughter, the dog and any bystanders.

The whole family is terrified by this manœuvre. Sophie and the dog are banned from the kitchen, Minna and Maurice shout at each other. The tension and Maurice's increasing deafness have increased the need for shouting, so that the kitchen becomes a roaring inferno. But so far there has never been an accident.

And then, at last, the turkey is ready – cooked, its bosom stuffed almost to bursting, the contents held by a glistening, crispy skin. But by this time Minna is done for, unable to eat. She must lie on the sofa during the carving period and try to recover her strength. And then she drags herself to the table.

Minna has lost her appetite. She is hot, exhausted and sick. She cannot serve the turkey. She sits slumped and sweating, fanning herself, while Selina puts everything on to plates. Now the sight of the dinner becomes offensive to Minna. She is nauseated by it. It brings back memories of her youth, of plucking and gutting poultry at an early age. Those few remaining bits of feather near the turkey's tail are the ones that turn her stomach. The thought of them. She feels the same about chicken feathers. She always singes them off.

A couple of years ago, to try and reduce Minna's workload, they all had dinner with the people upstairs. One Christmas dinner with Christians – a father, a mother and a grown-up son. They'd all been friends for years, swapped newspapers, played bridge, kept an eye on each other through illnesses and emergencies. But would the neighbours come up to scratch? They were to be responsible for vegetables, pudding and table arrangements. Everything would be eaten up there and Minna would only have to concentrate on the turkey.

It wasn't a totally successful experiment. The neighbours had overcooked the sprouts. And being Christians they had done everything properly, with tree, decorations, little presents and everyone having to wear funny hats.

This wasn't really Minna and Maurice's cup of tea. They couldn't relax properly. They couldn't go and lie down between the turkey and the pudding, or eat the pudding hours later, and as they both have digestive problems – wind, indigestion, hiatus hernia and general discomfort after large dinners – being unable to groan or stretch out was a bit of a strain. Then on top of that they had to read the jokes out of crackers and chat and say thank-you for the presents they didn't really like very much, and the potatoes weren't done in quite the way Maurice liked them and the whole thing took far longer than it needed to because etiquette takes time. Downstairs in their own flat they needn't have bothered with it.

Sophie and Selina liked having dinner upstairs. It made a change and the extra presents and crackers were a pleasant addition.

'Bloody waste of money,' snapped Minna afterwards, downstairs, referring to the crackers. 'Full of drek.' So they never did that again. And also, Aunty Zelda, now living round the corner, had to be sent a Christmas dinner. She lived alone and heated it up in her microwave. That year, when they all ate with the upstairs neighbours, Selina and Sophie tried another experiment. They made Aunty a turkey risotto, because the previous year she had been overloaded with roast turkey dinners. Her neighbour had sent her a large one round, which lasted two days, as well as Minna sending one over.

Expecting the same avalanche of roast lunches, and because Aunty was now unable to chew, Sophie, aged ten, thought of risotto. She loved it herself, called it Grisotto, helped to chop up all the bits and felt that she had invented it. Then they whizzed it over to Aunty's in the car, still hot. Meals on wheels.

Aunty Zelda was bitterly disappointed. She had wanted slices of roast turkey and gravy and roast potatoes, and of course, the stuffing, which couldn't be included in the Grisotto. That's what she'd been expecting – a proper Christmas dinner. The neighbours hadn't provided one either, by some quirk of fate.

That had been the year of experiments. This year Selina thought of another alternative. They should all go to an hotel for Christmas lunch. It would save an enormous amount of work. No one would get hot and worn out or be put off eating by the cooking.

Minna and Maurice hardly gave it a thought. In Maurice's opinion hotel food was sub-standard, compared to Minna's. The clientele might also prove an irritant. Hotels were out of the question. But Minna made one major concession. She would use tinned, ready peeled whole chestnuts instead of the fresh ones. It made very little difference to the stuffing. Everyone still loved it. Even Sophie, older and more sophisticated now, wanted some. It was also perfect cold, in sandwiches.

silent hill

tim hutchinson

For the first few mornings he found he could not breathe; the air was too sharp. In the cemetery the eldest gravestones were uprooted and piled up against the wall. Their windswept forms were too much at odds with the ordered philosophy of today's dead. The workmen had abandoned their digging because the ground had become too hard. Their shovels remained, sprouting like misshapen bows. The snow lay heavily on the gravestones.

They stood for a moment looking out across the lake. The tiny dark spot that had looked like a boat from the tower the other day was still there, motionless. Now they could see that it was a small island, a single punctuation in the vast ice desert. Off in the distance two factories emptied themselves into a cloudless sky. The smoke from the chimneys held there, frozen upright like an icicle. The air was so still that they could hear nothing, not even the faint voices of the people walking along the edge of the ice down below; there was no wind to carry even a whisper. He watched her as she made her way to the edge of the embankment, leaving footprints in the deep snow that had turned to ice overnight, caught by the sun like marble. To their left the woods encroached silently upon the lake, its boundary no longer defined, but dissolved imperceptibly into footstep pathways. The silver straight birches looked as if they had been tossed into the soil like javelins. It was a pure flat landscape.

The old wooden houses stood upon the lip of land squashed between the two lakes either side quietly resisting the slow pull of gravity, their façades small dashes of colour upon a white canvas. From this silent vantage point the morning opened out to him. He lingered for a moment breathing in one last time with his eyes as she turned and began to walk back down towards the large cross. As he followed he so wanted to look back over his shoulder; but the path was slippery and it took all his concentration to position his feet carefully. Before he realized it he was at the foot of the hill and the view had disappeared behind its lip; the moment had gone.

It felt curious, almost as if he had been planted in an imaginary Christmas. It was all here, all the right stuff. Snow, Christmas trees; this was after all the country where Father Christmas lived.

And yet it was all far too removed from his memory of Christmas. Dull sleet, old ladies getting excited on a bus at the sight of snowflakes. Christmas Day, not particularly cold, no intriguing sunset, no sun all day, no moon at night, drinking and eating and lonely in the longing. Always a need for something, for snow, for companionship, for food, for drink, for summer. Always a need for remembering, for talking, for assessing. A shallow fullness.

But here it was tremendously calming; slow, thoughtful, intellectual, considered, all the things that Christmas in London could never lay claim to. He had escaped the plastic tinsel, the sad lights, the huddle of bodies around the Selfridges windows. The fact of it was that an English Christmas artificially begun in October couldn't fail to disintegrate steadily into a pale December. It was like watching the pine needles collecting on the floor neath the tree in an ominous inevitable irritating pile.

But here it was different, almost a part of the landscape, a natural progression of the seasons. No shops, no pantos, nothing but a vast imperceptible landscape of imagery.

They walked in silence, down through the graves, irreverently peering into the holes in the ground, hoping to see a glimpse of a coffin, the suggestion of a body; passing one curious grave, covered with a steel lid; harsh, glinting, mirror-like, thick steam rising from beneath it in an attempt to thaw the ground for an addition.

Leaving the cemetery they walked briskly through the main

street, stopping only at the strange whining crossing beacons that beeped incessantly like flocks of gulls descending upon the town. Everyone did it, standing there even today when there was no traffic. It was absurd, especially when he remembered the confused mixture of bodies and metal that made up the roads at home. As they walked he peered into the shop windows finding a curious mixture of nostalgia and outdated technology, a gramophone and china, placed with hi-fi and Tupperware. As they neared the lake they crossed the bridge over the rapids that ran through the old textile mill, the water rushing through the core of the building, driving the machinery, steam rising violently as the icy water touched the red hot brickwork. As they continued between the tall factory mill and the opera house he felt as if he were at the mouth of a vast gorge, its sharp sides echoed in the curious architecture of the two contrasting buildings. In fact there was something curious about this whole town. It was as if it was no place at all, but a place constructed of memory. The mill from Black Country novels; the opera house from Paris, the trams from a London past, the architectural forms from Italy, the wooden cabins, the trees, the lakes, the snow from childhood memories of jigsaw puzzles he had received for Christmas presents.

He was cut off by language and so the voices around him became nothing but a deluge of sound, a stark contrast with the silent hill. Even the creases of clothing shouted, as people shuffled, conscious even of their footsteps, gently placing them upon ice. He was perplexed by this unfamiliarity. It was like watching TV with the sound turned off. He felt like a child again and faced with all these new things to see he smiled.

'What's up?' she said.

'Oh, nothing,' he replied. 'I was just remembering.'

The experience, the realization he could not even read the most banal of things on billboards, was wonderfully soporific. All at once his intelligence had been snatched away from him and a wonderful sense of inadequacy removed any last traces of responsibility.

Ducks were on the road. The pond in the park was frozen and

their tiny enclave, invaded by the ice, had thrown them into disarray, forcing them to widen their field in their search for food. The birds wandered aimlessly under their feet, refusing to move from the pathway cut by tramping boots in the snow. It was odd how one person walking, that first person, after the snow had fallen, should dictate the path of those to follow, as if their virgin footsteps held authority over the rest.

They turned from the park and almost immediately the town ceased as they passed an old wooden house, a memory of another age. Its windows smashed, its former colour visible only by the tiny flakings of paint still remnant in the cracking wood. And behind it they were engulfed by the trees. Intermittently as they walked they could see the pure white calm lake between the branches.

Then as they emerged from the wood he was overcome by a tremendous whiteness, an overpowering clarity that thrust itself into the far reaches of his mind. He stood absolutely transfixed, held there by the sensation of confusion deserting his body. Until eventually, released from this vision, he was able to make his first tentative step on to the ice. As his confidence grew his steps became more frequent and soon he found that they had walked out far from the land. It was unnerving to be detached like this; almost floating on a moment constructed by the physics of temperature.

He stood for a moment as the water boomed beneath them, the trapped air transporting the sound far away. They began walking out towards the centre. The sun was quite hot by now, reflecting the whiteness back up at their faces. He became entranced, separated from himself and lost in the pure endless expanse of the lake. He thought of what he had left behind; alleyways, winding streets, narrow chinks between buildings, evidence of human nature. He had left behind a country slave to the weather, slave to winter; to the leaves that fell on train tracks, to the water pipes that burst at the merest frost, to draughts, to shopping, to Christmas. He knew the house in London was full of people, and that wasn't him at all. He knew the awkward sense of polite invasion that was now filling its rooms.

Here was a straight pure clinical environment, where nothing existed but his own thoughts. She was beside him, walking. He desired nothing. It was Christmas Day. Already the sun had begun its early descent, pausing above the tree line, holding the day in suspension.

the gate of the year

frank tuohy

The young girl, daughter of one of the doctors, is carrying holly and paper chains. She is wearing a scarlet leather jacket and a miniskirt, because she is going on to a party.

There is a very old lady nestled in an armchair near the window. She looks up, furious. 'What does all this mean? Who are you? Who let you in? What are you doing here?'

The girl puts on a sunny smile: in a job like this, it helps to pretend you are on a TV show. 'Brought you some Christmas decorations. We're trying to liven up the place a bit. Mind if I use this chair?'

The girls stands on a chair and then a table. In the other rooms, old men have taken this opportunity to look up her skirts. The old lady is hunched up, silent, her lips and jaw moving as though chewing on an imaginary nut.

'There you are, Mrs – er –' On a holiday job, it's not really worth the trouble to learn their names. Then she remembers that this old dear is something special. 'All ready for Christmas. How many can you remember?'

This morning the girl learned that the old lady is a hundred years old. 'Why, that's wonderful.' 'Not wonderful for her,' the staff nurse said. 'Nor her children. She is using up all their savings.'

To the girl, then, the old lady looks sweet enough, but she's like a sort of Cookie Monster, eating money.

'Well, there you are then. Happy Christmas.'

The old lady says: 'Happy Christmas, dear.'

But she knows the girl is wrong. The wireless always told you when it was Christmas. If you could switch it on now, you'd know at once. You always listened in at Christmas, when Nelly was there. But the wireless set has disappeared or turned into something that might be an electric toaster, it is best not to experiment. The present is very confusing, but you only have to close your eyes and drop off to sleep for a few moments and everything clears up. Nobody is old in their own dreams: you are back in the gardens at Broadhurst with Nelly, or sitting on rugs on the lawn at St Miriam's, listening to dear, dear Miss Bickersteth reading poetry.

Nelly is often there at Christmas. Once, with Richard in the army in Egypt, and the two boys in Canada, you are alone together. She is still your very best friend, even though you have seen less of each other: you see her as she always was, not the stringy-looking child-less woman who always likes to make a fuss, but the little girl on the stairs at Vicarage Gate. Nowadays Nelly and her husband Cyril mostly live apart. She likes staying in hotels or nursing homes and in recent years took up, or was taken up by, a lot of new friends, who filled her conversation for a while and then obscurely vanished: Lady Fox and Miss Pargiter, Minna van Rentyen, Sister Hazelrigg and the Bousfield girls. None of them is mentioned this Christmas. You have to put up with the companionship of Alvar Liddell and John Snagge on the wireless. There's sherry before lunch and then roast chicken and mince pies, with more sherry, in front of a log fire. The recesses of the room are warmed by oil stoves, black objects with claw feet which throw cut-out patterns of light on the ceiling. Outside, rain and wind in the shrubberies, and a dozen laying hens waiting to be fed. At three o'clock the moment comes when you sit in a paroxysm of reverent embarrassment as that voice stumbles thickly onward. You feel so sorry for her. Is it the time when the quotation about 'the man who stood at the gate of the year' surprised everybody? Nelly doesn't know where it comes from, but then she is no reader, though good at crosswords. Then the national anthem. Two middle-aged ladies in tweeds rise to their feet and stand as strictly to attention as they ever did at roll call at St Miriam's.

That was the time you spent Christmas alone with Nelly, and she told you that she and Cyril would not be living together when the war is ended. She doesn't mind what happens to the house at Walton Heath: she has never liked it anyway. She will try to move to Ireland, where food is off the ration. You are shocked that she has become so hard and selfish, but you forgive her easily. She is your very best friend.

Besides, it all started long ago. It is Christmas at home, at Broadhurst, and Nelly is going to call in after church and introduce her fiancé. Though you're her very best friend, you've never met him or even seen a photograph.

This Christmas is going to be a very quiet one. Father has had his second stroke, and so it may well be the last Christmas here.

Broadhurst is an ugly Victorian house, secretly surrounded by conifers and other dark trees. In the eighties Father added on a billiard room and a nursery wing. In the girls' childhood, Father was already over sixty and he and his friends used to spend a lot of time shooting pheasants and in the evening they played billiards. In the upstairs corridor outside the night nursery you could hear the rumble of their voices and laughter. Girls weren't often allowed into the billiard room. Brother Ronald said that it was because Father and his friends liked to fart when they leaned over the billiard table to make a difficult shot; that was why they laughed such a lot of the time. That was the sort of horrid thing Ronald would say. He and Father have never got on, even before Ronald failed to get into Sandhurst, even before that business with the housemaids. Then the war came and he had a chance to make good, but a quite unsuitable woman got hold of him and they went through a form of marriage. Poor Godfrey had been miserable at Harrow because Mother had sent him in the clothes he'd had at private school, because there was still wear in them. He had been sent out East, and nobody had asked whether he would be happy there or not.

Father calls himself a 'free thinker' but he is quite content for his womenfolk to go to church. And so you drive Mother and Winifred to church, leaving Nurse Allardyce to look after Father. She has agreed to stay over Christmas, because travel is so difficult in wartime. It means that she will have to be there at meals but in wartime we must all be prepared to change our ways.

Mother is always in such a muddle about everything. When Winifred's nice Reggie came to Broadhurst for the first time, all she could think of saying was: 'I suppose you're after her money.' According to Winifred, Reggie answered: 'I didn't know she had any money,' but Mother pretended she had not heard. And now in the car Mother keeps saying: 'What shall we offer him? What do people drink at this time in the morning?'

You are sure it will be all right, because Nelly is still your best friend in spite of everything. In spite of Nelly having had other best friends, like Miss Margetson who taught art appreciation at St Miriam's, and Fräulein Schlimmer at the sanatorium in Switzerland where Nelly had to spend six months because of her lungs, and Miss Despard who taught Swedish exercises. When you were both at finishing school in Paris, Nelly was all over Mlle Dutourd, who took her twice to Fontainebleau, almost certainly without Mme Farrère's permission.

But everything is forgiven, you think, as you drive home from church and Mother keeps saying: 'Shall we have to offer sherry to Nurse Allardyce?' None of this matters because Nelly has found a man she can love. A car is parked in front of the porch and Nelly is there, neat, small, with her look of a fox-cub enhanced by a fur toque, fur muff, buttoned up against the cold winter air.

Cyril Acworth turns out to be large and rather stout, with pince-nez and a droopy moustache. He looks about fifty but is probably in his mid-thirties.

As soon as you can, you flee upstairs, and Winifred comes in to comfort you, as you cry out: 'How can she, how can she, that horrible-looking old man!'

Yet even after that, you are still the best of friends, the inseparable girls. Even when you yourself have found Richard, and try to explain to Nelly what a real marriage means. You are still friends now, even though Nelly has gone. You can't remember how or when that actually happened. In any case, you don't believe it is Christmas, so that it doesn't really matter. When Nelly is there it is the best of all Christmases.

The first time is at Granny's house. When you arrive in London at Euston station you have to take a cab to Granny's house in Vicarage Gate. Everyone does that when they get to London, which is dark and smells of soot and smoke; the sky seems low down over the rooftops. Mother has stayed at home this time, people have whispered but nobody has told you why, and Miss Hay, the governess, is arranging the cab, and while this is going on a rough man comes up, touching his cap. Miss Hay nods at him, he understands at once, and when the cab rattles off down the Marylebone Road you look out and the man is running along beside it. Then he disappears, you have lost him. In fact he has taken a short cut behind the Bayswater houses, through the mewses and narrow lanes.

When you arrive at Vicarage Gate, Granny herself comes out on to the front step. Though she is dressed all in black, with a black ribbon round her neck and some jet beads, she is still upright and young-looking. Father says that, unlike Mother, Granny knows how to deal with people. The man who has run all the way from Euston station now carries your trunks into the house. The breath coming and going in his chest makes a sawing noise. Granny deals with him, and he touches his cap and is swallowed up into the darkness.

In the hall, the gas bracket is popping gently. A grandfather clock faces a stuffed bird from India, which is ruffled and angry-looking. The smell of Granny's house is hot and rich, like curry. Uncle William and Aunt Bessie are there to welcome you, and a little girl follows them out of Granny's drawing room. She is dressed in the brown skirt and cream blouse which is going to be your uniform when you are at St Miriam's. You watch each other with the hostility of those whom their elders have designated to be friends.

Uncle William and Aunt Bessie are on leave, and they are looking after Nelly, whose parents are in India. Everyone is looked after by somebody. Mother and Father look after each other, Miss Hay looks after you at home, and also Ronald and Godfrey, though she complains they are getting beyond her control. At home there are a lot of rough men in the village, and fat women who shout from cottage doors, but Miss Hay or Mother is always there. Father looks after the girls who work in his factory: he makes them wear caps so that their hair doesn't get caught in the machinery.

In Granny's house the grown-ups open their presents on Christmas Eve and the children on Christmas morning. Uncle William has brought back large embroidered shawls from Kashmir. The wool they are made of is so fine that you can pass them through a wedding ring. Granny starts to take off her wedding ring to show how this is done, but you cry out for her to stop.

'What's wrong, dear?'

'Mother says that, if a lady takes off her wedding ring, her children disappear.'

Uncle William bursts out laughing at this. 'So you think I'll disappear?'

He is large and stout, and his stomach seems to be held in by his watch chain. And there's Aunt Bessie there too. You've heard it said that man and wife are one flesh, so perhaps she will disappear too.

So you say, to comfort them: 'No, I don't really believe it. It's just something I remember.'

And Nelly, who must believe sometimes that her parents have disappeared, goes off into peals of laughter. And you laugh too, and your friendship is there for ever.

Tomorrow will be Christmas Day and then you will get your presents. You lie there, with Nelly in the other bed, both of you still giggling from time to time. Miss Hay's supper has been brought up on a tray and you can hear her in the next room, munching and turning over the pages of the book she is reading, which is called *The Martyrdom of Man*. Outside in Kensington there is the sound of hansom cabs and horse buses. Uncle William has told you about a very rich man called Rothschild, who every Christmas sends a brace of pheasants to the drivers of the horse buses, and they hang them up beside their seats to ripen. Not very far away the underground train rattles its way between Kensington and Notting Hill Gate. And all these things are happening in the stodgy Edwardian dark, which will later seem like a photograph in sepia, but has its fair share of sunlight.

'Wake up, Mrs – er. It's your Christmas dinner.'

'Nelly darling, you got here after all.'

devaluation

mark kurlansky

It was one of those December mornings when Rosita Pineda was about to emerge. Nelcida Martínez Menea gazed past her weather-beaten shutters at Rosita's perfectly painted house. Turquoise with red trim, just like their house.

'The same paint, just fresher,' her husband, Danilo, had pointed out in that annoying way of his.

Nelcida's husband, Danilo, was standing in the street talking to Alvarita, the witch. Alvarita was fat like someone who wanted to show off how much she had to eat. She smiled to show her gold teeth. You did not want to know how she got the money for all that gold. Why, Nelcida wondered, was Danilo consulting the witch? She hoped it was a little powder to put in Rosita Pineda's turquoise and red freshly painted doorway. But she didn't think so. Rosita was their neighbor and their friend.

Danilo would not be wrong with a neighbor. He was a good man. Nelcida once again reflected on the fact that her husband was a good man, a better man than Rosita's husband who had run off to George Washington Hikes and, probably, no matter what Rosita said, had three women there and paid for them with cocaine. Everyone knew what went on.

Nelcida understood these things the same way she knew for certain that Rosita Pineda was about to come wriggling out of her freshly painted house. She would be wearing something new and it would be very tight, not because she wanted everything to be tight but because, according to Nelcida's theory, her husband in George Washington Hikes had not seen his wife in so long that he didn't know how fat she had become. This thought always made Nelcida laugh until Rosita came out and Nelcida was forced to admit that Rosita was one of those lucky women who only got fat in her bottom which was exactly where men wanted you to be fat. Once Rosita was walking away from them in her New York clothing and Nelcida noticed her good husband, Danilo, looking after her, his eyes clearly focused on the fattest part, one eye on each.

Nelcida didn't have Rosita's luck. If she got fat it would all be in her stomach. But Rosita didn't have a good man like she did.

And now Rosita did emerge as predicted wearing something tight and new and bright blue that shone across her bottom. It was December and she was starting to get the packages. Every December she would get packages from New York filled with clothes that were too small for her and more electronic games for their children – boxes and tubes and consoles and remote-controlled airplanes, cars, trucks and boats. Their two-room house was furnished with these things. There was no other table space. If Rosita wanted to put out a dish of mangoes she had to put it on an electronic machine. When she laid out her New York clothes to decide what to wear she had to lay them over electronic machines.

Nelcida and Danilo and the other neighbors didn't know exactly what any of these devices did. Most of them did nothing most of the time because there was no electricity. But everything was always kept plugged in and sometimes at about ten in the evening the electricity would miraculously kick on. Everybody knew the exact moment more from sound than sight. Some lights would come on. There were three street lights on their block which, by the way, was a paved block. But the main thing that happened when the electricity came was that Rosita Pineda's house came alive with strange electronic beeps, bleeps, buzzes and burps. And there was something that played the first three bars of *La Cucaracha*.

The reason Nelcida had known that Rosita was about to emerge was that a package had come. Everyone had seen it delivered by a man on a motorscooter. Now she would have to come out and smile at everyone and talk about the weather before adding, 'Oh and I heard from Rafael!'

'Oh well,' Nelcida thought. 'She has bad hair. She probably had Haitians in her family.' Nelcida took her position by the weather-beaten shutter brushing her own smooth Spanish hair so that Rosita, as she did her rounds, could see the difference.

Danilo had not wanted to talk to Alvarita at all but, because she was a witch, she could see his secrets. If someone like that wants to talk to you, you can't ignore them. Danilo had a bad tooth. He had felt it coming a few weeks ago. First his teeth all felt a little out of line like they do when you have been punched in the mouth. Then came the ache and sometimes a throb and sometimes it would travel up the entire side of his face and jab in somewhere at the underpart of his brain so he could not think. He should get someone to pull it. Luis Manuel wanted a hundred and fifty pesos to do it. That was the way everything was getting to be. One week's salary just for one tooth. If it were in the front he could have done it himself.

It would have to wait until he had bought his family Christmas presents. He had to do that fast because everybody said they were going to devalue the peso again. If they devalued the peso he would never be able to buy Christmas presents. Rosita would be next door with presents. Her children would have more gadgets and Sonia on the other side would have presents for her children because her man was in Puerto Rico sending money and Nelcida and their children would have nothing, or maybe worse, Dominican things, because that was the best he could do.

His tooth felt like a metal bar wedged inside somewhere pressing against his face. All he wanted right now was to get out to the cane fields and get a cool glass of green cane juice. Danilo had been virtually suckled on sugar and it comforted him. The village he came from in the Cordilleras had no milk. All the babies were given sugar and water. It was as good as milk. When his children needed milk he could pay for it. But that was before the devaluations. If he had a

baby now he would probably give it sugar. Sugar soothed everything, even his tooth.

But first he had to talk to Alvarita. Since he could not get his tooth
pulled he did not tell anybody about it. But Alvarita could see it. He
wanted her to give him some kind of leaf or powder to stop the pain
but Alvarita said that she could see that there was nothing wrong
with the tooth. 'It's a sign.'

'A sign of what?'

And in a low raspy voice she said, 'a *curse*.' She always said it like
that. She could never say the word curse normally. She liked to scare
people. It was a way of controlling them. He was a policeman so he
understood.

'You will never get rid of it by losing the tooth. You have to lose
. . the *curse*.' According to Alvarita the only hope was to kill a cat and
she made a motion with her fat hands like opening a stiff jar lid
which was supposed to mean twisting a cat's head off which, it
seemed to Danilo, was probably impossible to do.

He passed Beni and his brother. Beni's brother was nineteen and
muscular with skin the color of good leather and always had a stack
of pesos that he counted in silence as though daring someone to take
it away from him. Beni was nine years old, small and cheerful. He
always said, 'Hey Danilo, good luck today.' Then he winked. Beni
was a nice kid but Danilo didn't like the wink. He knew Beni worked
with the army, and though he knew Beni hated them for taking his
money, you couldn't trust somebody who worked with the army.

He was the last to get to the post because he had to get the cane
juice which he swirled around his tooth and held in his cheek until
he had only a vague ache. It was a good post, a broad traffic circle on
the highway between Santo Domingo and San Pedro de Macorís.
Everyone who went to the Free Zone had to go that way and they
would come flying through that good straight flat road past the cane
fields, looking like one of Alvarita's curses, with the yellowish smoke
from the harvesting cane fields circling furiously in the headlights to
part for the oncoming car and then, suddenly, with no warning, the
car would hit the circle and the tires would moan as the driver down-

shifted to make the curve. Then, when he was all slowed down, they had him.

Danilo or one of his two partners would go out on to the road and motion for the car to stop. Sometimes the car kept going. Danilo and his partners were not about to waste their gasoline chasing after it. They sat and waited in the circle surrounded by the cane fires whose smoke smelled like vegetables roasting in caramel and tried to flag down the slow ones. At the end of the day they siphoned off the gas they had not used and sold it. They would get more gas from the police garage. The whole beauty of this spot was that cars had to slow down so it was easy to stop them.

There was always something not quite right about Danilo, his partners thought. He didn't even want to do the speeding ticket business until after the second peso devaluation. He must have been the last one in the department. When Danilo's partners stopped someone they would tell the driver he was speeding and tell him he had to pay a two hundred peso fine. Sometimes the driver would pay it but usually he would just hand over fifty or a hundred pesos. Sometimes the driver would argue and it would get into bartering. 'No more than fifty pesos.'

'I'm sorry sir, the fine is two hundred pesos.'

'Here, take a hundred.'

They would always take it.

Danilo had a different way of operating. He would stop the car and say, 'You were speeding, let me see your license please.' He stared very intensely at the driver's license comparing the photo with the actual face, back and forth as though there were a checklist. Eyes, two. Check. Nose, one. This always softened them up. It was just like the way Alvarita said '*curse*.'

Then he would say, 'You have to pay a fine.'

Up to this point Danilo's partners admired his work but this was the part that really provoked them. The driver would ask how much the fine was and Danilo would always say, 'It's Christmas time. I have three children. Give what you can.' And they would give anything from a few coins to a few hundred pesos.

His partners did Danilo impressions. This little nasal voice pleading: 'It's Christmas time, give what you can.'

'Jesus Christ Danilo!' they would shout as the driver left. 'We're
suppose to be the fucking cops!'

But Danilo always argued that it was important not to get
anybody angry. 'They could make a complaint. If they make a complaint the army hears about it. If the army hears about it, you know
what happens.'

They did know. If the army learns about a good spot they take it
away from the police and use it themselves. Danilo and his friends
had paid two thousand pesos for this spot.

Only Danilo was trying to buy Christmas presents for his family.
To his partners this was further evidence that Danilo was not quite
right. It was normal for cops to grab a little extra in December for
Christmas with their family but a beautiful spot like this that cost the
three of them a real investment – who would use that for Christmas
presents? They were going to leave and get work in dollars and send
it back. Danilo should do that too. 'Next year your family can have
lots of presents,' they would say. 'And you won't have to worry
about devaluations either. The lower they drop the peso, the richer
you get. Think about that.'

Danilo would say, 'Listen, do what you want. You go somewhere
else and you are as good as a Haitian. You have to stay in your
country and work and give things to your family.'

Danilo knew exactly what to buy with the money. First of all
Nelcida would get something blue. It had to be blue. He saw that this
morning. And the boys would get battery-operated toys. Things
that worked without electricity. Their house would buzz even
during the blackouts. And the youngest boy would get an M-16 he
saw. If he could get it before the devaluation it would only be two
hundred and forty pesos. It looked exactly like the real M-16s that
the army sons-of-bitches had. And it came with three clips that you
could put in and take out. His youngest boy wanted an M-16 ever
since Danilo had told him how the boy's grandfather had been shot
in the foot with one by an American Marine in 1964.

On Kings' Day when Dánilo was giving his family presents, his partners would have to have already gotten across the passage. In January the sea got too rough to cross. Before then they had to raise enough money to pay for the *yola* and have enough left so their families would be all right if they didn't get anything to them for a while. They spent most of the day arguing about how to tell a good *yola* from a bad *yola* and what was a fair price. 'Never make a deal with a green-eyed *yola* man. You will end up at the bottom of the sea,' one said.

'Just make sure they don't have tar on their pants. It shows they have been patching the boat.'

'You want someone who doesn't patch his boat?'

Another topic was whether to stay in Puerto Rico or go on to New York.

'You can make good money in Puerto Rico.'

'You make better money in New York, asshole.'

'You go to New York and you are spit on by Puerto Ricans.'

'So, you think you aren't spit on by Puerto Ricans in Puerto Rico, you faggot.'

'So, dumb shit, why travel all the way to New York to earn dollars and get spit on by Puerto Ricans when you can do both just on the next island!'

The two would get so involved in these debates that they would seldom notice an oncoming car and invariably Danilo would be left to flag down the car and go through his procedure. Then the others would hoot and start doing their Danilo impressions.

Sam Elis was happy to be back. He loved this place. When people asked him, he could never explain it. Sometimes he thought it was just that he was the only one. No matter how squalid and miserable Haiti got, everybody loved it. Shouldn't someone cross over and love this place too? Sam Elis did. He was first here as a political science student and had since come as a human rights advocate, an adviser to an urban planning firm, an election observer. But it was getting harder every time. He hadn't been down in more than a year when he learned that a group of North American union leaders wanted a report on labor conditions in the Free Zones.

The union leaders had not given him much of a budget. The urban planners had been better. Now he had to stretch out a small stipend twice as far as intended. It would take time to find out what was really going on in these Free Zones. He wasn't going to do a quick job, just because the budget was small.

For the moment he was just wandering on foot in the old colonial zone enjoying being back. For lunch he would go down to the Malecon and have crabs and rice and beer for only fifty pesos. With the devaluation it was less expensive than last year. That was one break in his favor anyway.

Beni's brother walked up alongside of Sam Elis and whispered nervously, 'You want to buy pesos?'

Elis waved him away.

'I'll give you fifteen hundred.'

Last time he went for crabs and rice on the Malecon it was thirty pesos which cost him about seven twenty-five. Now it was fifty pesos.

He couldn't calculate right now because Beni's brother was whispering numbers in his ear.

'How much for fifty?' Elis asked.

'Sorry; there is a one hundred minimum.'

Sam wanted to see how this worked before he put out too much money. But he liked this kid with his minimum. He made him laugh.

'What are you, American Express?'

Beni's brother laughed. 'Do it for three or four hundred,' he said, patting Sam on the back. 'You stay around here? How long are you staying?'

Sam loved these people. 'OK, I'll change two hundred for thirty-two hundred pesos.'

'Thirty-one hundred!' Beni's brother protested.

'No, thirty-two or nothing,' Sam insisted.

'Shit,' said Beni's brother. 'You guys . . . OK, let me see the two hundred. How long are you staying?'

'Let's see the thirty-two hundred pesos,' said Sam.

Reluctantly Beni's brother took out his thick stack of pesos and skillfully counted out thirty-two one-hundred peso notes, folded them over with professional finesse and handed them to Sam who counted them again while Beni's brother tried one more time. 'You staying here long?'

Sam Elis took out four fifty-dollar bills and handed them to Beni's brother just as Beni came running down the quiet old colonial street rebuilt for tourists who had not come. 'Mister, Mister!' shouted Beni almost out of breath. Then he turned to his brother. 'You are so stupid. Are you crazy standing here changing money. The army is coming.' Indeed there were a number of bored soldiers in green dragging weapons like they were mops, drifting their way.

'Maybe this is not a good idea,' said Sam. 'We stood here too long.'

'You are still standing here!' Beni whispered hoarsely. 'This is stupid.' Sam suddenly realized how foolish he would look criticizing Free Zone management if he were arrested for black market money changing so he slipped the pesos back to Beni's brother and Beni's brother slipped the dollars back to Sam. 'Maybe later,' said Beni's brother as they both shoved their own money back in their pockets. 'How long are you staying?'

'I don't know. A while.'

'Come on!' said Beni pointing at the soldiers. Beni's brother and Sam Elis walked quickly in opposite directions leaving Beni standing there.

By the time Beni and his brother met with the army to give them their 20 per cent, Sam Elis was back in his hotel examining the one-dollar bill with one-peso bills folded inside.

Beni's brother took out a fifty-dollar bill and a ten-dollar bill. He showed the lieutenant the fifty-dollar bill and handed him the ten-dollar bill saying, 'I got fifty off of him.' The lieutenant slapped him on the left ear. 'You think I am stupid.' He grabbed Beni's brother by the right wrist and walked away with both bills.

'Shit,' said Beni's brother rubbing his ear. Beni reached up and patted his brother on the back. 'That's the problem with the military. You know that. They're not honest, the fucking military. That's what's wrong with this fucked country. You know that.' There was a siren in his left ear. He only heard Beni's voice as though in the distance from the other side of his head.

It was dark and the electricity had not yet come on when Danilo got back to the neighborhood swishing fresh cool green cane juice in his mouth from a thin plastic cup. A slight rustle in the trees, the hum of a few men's voices talking in the street and the occasional clang of a pot, a baby's wail gathering force like a hand cranked siren – these sounds stood out because it seemed so quiet in the dark.

It had not been a bad day. When they split everything three ways, including the gasoline they sold off – almost a full tank – they had so far brought in enough to earn back their investment. Tomorrow would be the day they would begin making a profit. His tooth made him feel like his whole mouth was being crushed and distorted. Profits. He felt almost certain if he looked in a mirror he would find his mouth completely askew. Tomorrow the profits would start. If only there would not be a devaluation, not just yet. He wondered if Alvarita knew how to stop a devaluation.

Nelcida was trying to cook dinner on a charcoal grill. The bottled gas they had been using had gotten too expensive for a policeman's salary. They were back to charcoal or even wood, just like in the mountain village where Danilo was born. He remembered his excitement when he had heard that in the capital, where they were going, people cooked with gas. He could not imagine what gas was. His mother had explained that it was something that burned but you couldn't see it. One of the wonders of the capital, now vanished, through devaluation.

Five minutes of rain at six o'clock had been just enough to find every loose seam in the tin roof and the charcoal had somehow gotten wet and would not burn. 'Maybe there is some wood in the neighborhood,' Danilo suggested.

Nelcida looked over at Rosita Pineda's freshly painted house, so shiny that even in the dull moonlight of this cloudy evening there was no missing the fact that it was fresh paint. 'Maybe Rosita has wood.'

'Only plastic. It's all plastic.'

'She should tell her man in George Washington Hikes to send machines made out of wood next year. Then they could be used for something.' She smiled triumphantly but her joke was ruined by a glimpse of Rosita in her house. She was cooking on a gas burner.

Danilo went out to the paved street where the men leaned against the lamp posts and passed the dark quiet evening whispering. No one felt like talking in a full voice with the electricity out. It seemed like they tried to go easy on their own energy until the power came back.

The reason that the street was paved and had three street lights on tall metal posts was that the street backed the government. No matter how bad things got in this government neighborhood, as the men stood in the dark and talked about the prices, the devaluations, the blackouts, the shortages (sometimes it was even hard to find sugar in the stores), sooner or later someone would scrape his shoe along the black top and say, 'Well, he paved the road.' It started as a serious point, then it became a joke, now it was just something you said, a meaningless traditional refrain. They had moved on to other jokes like smacking the metal post of the unlit street light and saying, 'He gave us something to lean against anyway.'

Suddenly there was a whirring noise, and the throb of a distant meringue, and blops and beeps and *La Cucaracha* from the Pineda house where purple and orange lights flashed and tiny little vehicles left their ports and zipped across the wooden floor and crashed into walls. Bare white light bulbs illuminated the green interiors of the houses and two of the three street lights came on and – most important of all – fans started blowing air. The men returned to their homes to enjoy a few hours of electricity. Danilo had been thinking that if Christmas went all right and he could keep the good spot perhaps he could buy a gasoline generator and run it off of the gas he siphoned instead of selling it at the end of the day.

The electricity lasted only thirty minutes that night and Danilo's tooth would not let him sleep. In the morning he passed Alvarita without speaking. She just puffed up one cheek, pointed to it, made a meowing noise and then twisted her fist and clicked her tongue like the sound of something snapping.

Sam Elis didn't even allow himself to think about the two hundred dollars he had stupidly lost. He would make it up in other ways. He rented the cheapest car he could find, a powder blue light-weight pick-up truck from a local rental agency. The local press had gotten interested in his project and he was giving interviews, partic-ularly bearing down on one shadowy figure named E.J.Tyler who had opened up three different assembly operations in the past six months. In one plant where they had demanded he lower the quota for overtime he had fired all three hundred workers. He said he lost his contracts. A week later he announced new contracts and hired a different three hundred women.

E.J.Tyler did not like Sam Elis who he had never met. He read the newspapers. It made him angry and he called some friends in government and arranged to deliver a speech entitled 'Free Zones, the engine of Dominican development.' Then he got into his rental car, rolled up the windows, turned the air-conditioning up full and sped off to San Pedro. The day before, he had been stopped for speeding. The cop had wanted two hundred pesos but seemed happy with one hundred. With all the devaluations one hundred pesos was nothing and it seemed he would be stopped no matter what speed he went. So he might as well go as fast as he wanted.

Danilo could not concentrate on his work. The cane juice wasn't working. The electricity had been off too long and the juice vendor had no way to keep it cold. He buried it in the field by the side of the road and hoped the ground would keep it cool siphoning it up through a rubber hose, exactly like they did with the gasoline. He even spit out the first mouthful when he primed the tube. But the lukewarm cane juice did not help Danilo's tooth.

Normally, in Danilo's line of work, when you see a big waxed rental car like E.J.Tyler's rocketing toward you, you jump into action. These were the kind of cars that paid. But something else caught Danilo's attention as he stood in the circle, his tooth feeling like a dull edged screwdriver were jammed in his jaw, watching E.J.Tyler's big car push away the cane smoke and shoot toward him. From out of the cane field came – was it a mongoose? – no, a cat, a black cat running right out in the road in front of the fast cruising rental car. The cat stopped a fraction of a moment to assess and then made the remarkably bad decision to try and make it across, reaching with his body in huge strides then snapping together and reaching again, stretching his elastic stride right in front of the new thick treaded tires.

'Would this count?' Danilo wondered and crossed himself and hoped for the worst.

But as though the cat were only made of air he just kept going and disappeared into the field on the other side of the road as the car squealed around the circle, downshifted and got back on the straightaway to San Pedro.

'Hey Danilo, you sleeping?' said one of his partners. The two partners were lounging in the car slouched down, the doors opened, debating unlucky numbers. 'I'm just saying, if you don't want to end up on the bottom, don't get on a *yola* on the seventh, fourteenth or twenty-first.'

'Listen,' said Danilo. 'I have a problem with a bad tooth. Why don't one of you take the next one?'

'You take the next one. We will take the one after.'

The next one was perfect. A good quality rental car driving slowly down the highway. The ideal candidate for a speeding ticket. Danilo signaled him to stop. When he did his routine the driver looked at him angrily and said, 'Give what I can! You mean you want a bribe!'

'No sir,' insisted Danilo, feeling threatened. 'We are not allowed to take bribes. This is a speeding ticket.'

'In cash?'

'Yes, please.'

'So it's a Goddamn bribe. Here take a hundred-peso bribe. I don't care.'

'No sir, I cannot accept a bribe. Only a –'

And at that second the driver snapped the hundred-peso bill out of sight and said, 'Fine. Don't take a bribe,' and put his car into gear and left.

Danilo's two partners started smacking their heads with their hats in comic frustration. 'Danilo, Danilo, Christ Almighty.' And they went into Danilo impressions. 'OOHH!! No, I can't take a fucking bribe!'

Danilo explained that they had to be careful with people like that, but his partners weren't listening. They would take the next car. The next car didn't look very promising. It was traveling slowly enough but it looked like a local truck, just some little powder blue pick-up truck. They wouldn't have stopped it at all except that it was going so slowly that they had time to see that the driver was a Yanqui. They weren't going to take less than two hundred pesos. They had to show Danilo how to do it.

Sam Elis thought, this is exactly the kind of thing that is rotting this country. It's everywhere and people have to start saying no. So he refused to pay.

'If you don't pay you will be arrested.'

'Good and you can go to the US Embassy with your superior and explain all about the two hundred pesos. I wasn't even driving fast.'

'I say you were.'

'Fine, you tell your story and I will tell mine.' He crunched the stick shift until he found first gear and drove off.

'Those are exactly the kind of Yanquis you have to be careful about,' said Danilo.

Three mornings later Danilo was leaving for work and Beni, instead of winking and wishing him good luck, reached up to pat Danilo's shoulder. 'Hey listen, I think I heard something. Some Yanqui complained. This one sounded really interesting to the sons-of-bitches in the army. I think they were talking about your spot.'

So that was it. He had warned his partners. He knew exactly which Yanqui it was. Never stop a Yanqui with a bad car. Alvarita was probably right. He probably was cursed. The devaluation would probably come today too.

They worked hard that day thinking it could be their last chance. At three in the afternoon they stopped one of those big expensive rentals. He was going fast but now they were even stopping speeders. Danilo stuck to his proven technique. 'It's Christmas, if you could just give whatever you can. I have four children.' (He added the fourth for effect. He was desperate.)

'Is that right,' said E.J.Tyler. 'And those two are your partners? Why don't you bring them over here.' While Danilo was talking his two partners into getting out of the patrol car, E.J.Tyler fumbled underneath his new *guayabera* for his wallet. He handed two one-hundred-dollar bills to each of the three of them, wished them Merry Christmas, and then, as an afterthought, gave each of them one of his business cards. As he drove off he thought to himself, 'No son-of-a-bitch is going to go around this country – my fucking island – calling me a cheap bastard.' The rental car soon vanished as though swallowed by the cane smoke.

A few days later Danilo's partners were gone and Danilo was reassigned in the capital. He drove by the spot one day and saw the army was there. But it didn't matter. US dollars were devaluation proof. And Beni could get him a good price on pesos. He bought boxes of presents for his family. The one disappointment was that there were no more M-16s and he had to settle for one with curved clips. The salesman explained they were better. 'The Cubans use them.' But his father wasn't shot in the foot by a Cuban and he couldn't tell the boy that this was the same kind of gun with which they shot Grandpa in the foot.

Still he had done it. He even got his tooth pulled by Luis Manuel for a hundred and fifty pesos which only cost him eight dollars. It was like being a Yanqui. And there he was, a Dominican man, still living in the Dominican with his family bringing home presents for Christmas. He felt like a man, like the way his father felt in the days when he could grow crops.

Nelcida was trying to start the meal fanning the charcoal. They weren't making the charcoal right any more. It just didn't burn right. She could see Rosita, the frizzled nest of bad hair glowing blue in the light of the gas burner where she was cooking her dinner. 'Danilo, how much money do you make in George Washington Hikes?'

'Who knows.'

'I wonder how much you could save if you went there for just maybe six months.'

Danilo felt a sting like when he was a boy and his mother slapped him. He walked over to her. 'Would you want to be like these other woman without your man here looking after things?'

'No, Danilo. You are a good man,' said Nelcida Martínez Menea as she gazed past her weatherbeaten shutters at the perfectly painted house of Rosita Pineda.

the mexican christmas tree

miriam frank

Ruth was trying to figure out new faces on the marble pattern of the floor tiles, while she sat swinging her legs from the rim of the old iron bathtub. Over the few months they had lived in that apartment, she had come to know every wriggle and smudge on that floor. There, a dog about to sit down with half its tail missing emerged from the tile in the corner while, beyond her right foot, an odd face with pointed beard and wild hair stared back at her. But that evening she was waiting with nothing to do, and she was beginning to feel impatient. She glanced around to find something new on which to fix her attention, but the evenly placed tiles on the wall gleamed a uniform white in the light of the single naked bulb that hung from the middle of the ceiling, and she already knew their every chip and crack. She slid down from the edge of the bathtub and walked towards the door.

'Can I come out yet?'

'No! Not yet! It'll soon be ready.'

Her mother's voice was tender and reassuring. Everything had moved and altered in Ruth's short life, which had filed past her in a kaleidoscopic procession of homes, townscapes, country roads, people and impressions. Everything, that is, except her mother. She had always been there: her warm, moist smell, the firm grip of her hand when they walked side by side in new streets and places, her decisiveness and clarity amid the often puzzling events around them. And that had made Ruth feel comfortable and confident in a world that was forever changing around her.

Occasional sounds of rustling movements and of footsteps alternating with silent intervals reached her from the other side of the bathroom door. Her curiosity was growing along with her impatience: what could her mother be up to? She had never had to wait in the bathroom like this before. There was going to be a surprise, her mother had said. Ruth stood at the door carefully listening for any clues, her head barely reaching above the doorknob. Gingerly, she leant forward and peeped through the keyhole . . . and gasped with astonishment. On the mirror in the hallway, was the dazzling reflection of a brightly decorated tree. It was covered by a scintillating mass of coloured balls, gold and silver tinsel, and a myriad of small objects which she could not distinguish from her side of the bathroom door, turning the tree into a brilliant image on the mirror! She also managed to catch glimpses of her mother who was standing on one side teasing out fine strands of cotton wool and placing them carefully on the branches, giving the tree the semblance of having been in a fresh snowfall.

'You can come out now, Ruth!' she heard her mother call out excitedly.

Ruth turned the doorknob and at last found herself standing in front of the tree. Silently, she took in and carefully savoured the whole sight, and then slowly started examining each individual detail: shiny red and blue baubles, sparkling tinsel dripping from the branches, curly candles with dancing orange flames, little angels with golden trumpets, chocolates in glittery foil, toy birds with pink and purple feathers, tinkly bells, gilded walnuts, silvery stars, all of these and more dangled from the 'snow' daubed branches of the laden fir tree . . . and underneath the lowest branches, stacked on the floor, she now noticed a large pile of presents.

'Who are they for?'

'For you!'

'For me? All of them?'

Her mother watched her with a happy smile and Ruth sensed her mother's pleasure at her own surprise and delight. Lisa, a young woman who had travelled on the same ship and, since their arrival, shared the apartment with them although Ruth hardly ever saw her, was also there this evening. She was standing in the hallway on the other side of the tree watching and enjoying the girl's excitement too.

Ruth went up to the tree and squatted in front of the pile of toys to have a closer look at them. On top of the heap were two pink celluloid dolls, their heads and limbs slightly flexed, the girl doll dressed in a little white blouse with red piping and a blue checked skirt, white cotton socks and black shoes, and the boy, a red shirt, short blue trousers, and similar socks and shoes. Timidly, she picked them up and held them in front of her, looked at them intently and then slowly turned them over to examine them back and sides, lifted the girl's skirt to find a little pair of white cotton pants under it, and pulled up the boy's shirt to look at his tummy which had a dimple for a belly button.

'What are their names?'

'They're your dolls. You think up a name for them.'

'I will call them Juanito and Juanita,' Ruth decided instantly, recalling the names of her favourite friends in the small Spanish town where they had lived in a big house with a garden, though those memories had by now merged with her mother's accounts of their life there, where hers had started.

In the pile of presents, she also found a game with a chequered square board and a set of red and blue pieces, a Walt Disney book with lovely pictures, and a skipping rope. She had never received so many toys all at once before. She remembered the chocolates her mother had given her in Marseilles from Santa Claus, or *Père Noël* as she had known him there. Their unusual curly shapes and fluted paper wrappers had been proof of his existence, had she needed any! But apart from those chocolates, that magic old man in red with a long white beard had not had occasion to leave her any other presents before, either in Marseilles, the last place they had lived in before coming here – in that small, dark room where friends came and went at all hours and had long conversations with her mother of the sort grown-ups had, keeping their voices down as though wishing not to be heard outside – nor in the various other French towns and villages in which they had stayed for short periods with people she didn't know but who had been very kind, who had shared their meals at their tables with them and given them beds for the night in between endless journeys with an old suitcase in rickety old buses. But now they were here, in this new country, Mexico, and since their arrival Ruth had been busy taking everything in: the new cityscapes of skyscrapers and colourful lit-up signs of Corona beer and Pepsi Cola, the streets where the incessant tooting and beeping of cars intermingled with the cries of newspaper boys, the strange aromatic and acrid street smells of warm tortillas, *jícamas* with hot chile, charred corn on the cob and all kinds of fruits she had never seen before. A hotter sun, more drenching downpours, sheets of lightning followed by the deafening rumble of thunder, a ground that twice had suddenly and without warning quaked violently under her feet. She was busy relearning Spanish, becoming acquainted with new people, and adjusting to a large school full of children who seemed to think of her as different. It was an entirely new life once again, and at the same time a continuation of the changing world that she had by now grown used to expect.

She had been too busy with her present to look back or think about the past. Even the immediate past still vivid in her memory was receding rapidly and she was thinking less and less of the old friends they had left behind. It had all started in the small town in northern Spain which her parents had chosen when they had been obliged to leave their native Germany, and where Ruth's first years had been carefree and happy surrounded by family and friends in that large country house which she still retained in some corner of her memory. That was, until the day they were dispersed by Franco's advancing armies and ended up across the border where their flight was resumed, this time from the Vichy French and the occupying Germans, resulting in a continuous series of moves which Ruth had found inexplicable but had accepted as the natural course of events.

But on this particular evening Ruth's whole attention was focused on that glowing, brilliant image before her, tinsel and stars, shiny red and blue balls, angels and candles, chocolates and toys, enveloping, dangling from, and sitting under the tree. Ruth was experiencing an entirely new sensation, a thrill of pleasure coupled with surprise, the excitement of unexpected presents that perhaps she would not have to give up or leave behind very soon. But maybe the most delicious sensation of all was simply the joy of the occasion which she was sharing with her mother and Lisa in the warmth and security of their small apartment on the top floor of the building. And nothing, then, could have been further from Ruth's thoughts than the friends who had not come with them. Friends who probably – at that very moment – were being hunted and caught, starved and tortured, faced by human indifference and brutality, some perhaps already dead from a bullet or a beating, on that icy Christmas Eve on the other side of the Atlantic where they had just come from . . .

Ruth was six when she saw her first Christmas tree. Every year after that, her mother prepared and decorated another tree for Ruth to enjoy in her native German tradition which had enchanted children since medieval times, when the Tree of Paradise – as it was then called – was decorated with apples, and further back to pre-Christian times when the evergreen fir tree was celebrated in mid-winter as a symbol of eternal life. For Ruth, the candles carefully clipped on to its outer branches made it glow with magic, the fluffy cotton-wool strands draped on its branches looked like real snow, and under the tree she always found a pile of presents. The tree brought them together, it was the focus of a shared, happy evening, one time in the year when her mother wasn't out or busy or worried, when Ruth and her mother both had time to consider and talk to one another. A time of mutual recognition around the tree. Santa Claus had something to do with it, surely the tinsel and small toys that hung from its branches were from him. But up till now, Ruth had not heard of Jesus Christ, neither in their life of survival in France, nor during their early times in Mexico. Her mother often spoke to her about her grandparents who had stayed behind in Germany, her father who couldn't come with them, and her uncles, aunts and cousins who had found new homes in other countries and were now spread out in all five continents. She sometimes referred to her happy, normal life before it was disrupted by the events that led to the war, and mentioned her friends and their shared hopes and work together for a friendlier world, now shattered. And as Ruth gradually grew more aware of all these things, she lost that sheer, unguarded pleasure she had felt with her first Christmas tree: the troubled world around her had found its way into her consciousness and she was no longer able ever to forget it completely.

As they settled into their new life in Mexico and Ruth made new friends, she was also invited to take part in their Christmas *posadas*. Everyone gathered together and, each holding a burning candle, the women with their shawls draped over their heads, walked down the street and stopped at every door to sing the verses of a long ballad-like arrangement of questions and answers. The group outside the door represented the holy couple asking for shelter, while the people inside the house played the part of the innkeeper giving his answers.

(The group outside)	(The group inside)
In the name of Heaven	This isn't an inn
please give us shelter	continue on your road
for my beloved bride	I can't open up
can walk no further.	for you might be a rogue.
Don't be so inhuman	Be off on your way
show us some mercy	and stop molesting
and God in Heaven	for if you make me cross
will surely reward thee.	I'll give you a thrashing.

And so on. Many more verses were sung back and forth between the two groups until the innkeeper finally let the holy couple in:

May God repay you	Blessed be the house
for your goodwill	which this day gives refuge
may Heaven overwhelm you	to the immaculate Virgin
with joy to your fill.	to Mary so beauteous.

Once inside, they would all congregate around and admire a miniature model of the Nativity made up of a stable with real straw
covered with a roof made of sticks. Small, detailed terracotta figures
of Joseph and Mary, the three kings dressed in brightly coloured
clothes holding their offerings, and the stable animals which
included cows, donkeys, horses, sheep, pigs and ducks, all stood in
silence around the central little manger where the baby Jesus lay. On
the stick roof, a golden terracotta angel stood guard.

Then the party would start with brightly decorated *piñatas* which
the children took turns to break, blindfolded, with a stick, followed
by the scramble after its spilt contents of sweets, peanuts and small
toys all over the floor. Noisy fireworks, a grand meal with hot chile
and *tortillas*, and lively and happy dancing to their Latin American
rhythms would continue long into the night. The *posadas* were part
of that mysterious Roman Catholic world of Ruth's school friends.

Three years after her first Christmas tree, the war in Europe
ended. There was tremendous excitement and joy. But Ruth also
witnessed her mother's anxiety and grief as she scanned the long lists
of names that began to arrive regularly with the post, now and then
coming across those of relatives and friends. They were the dead of
the concentration camps.

They returned to Europe and settled in England. Ruth grew up and
married and eventually had children of her own. Now it was her turn
to decorate a tree every Christmas Eve and pile all the presents for
her children under it. She noted with interest that the English Santa,
or Father Christmas as he was known here, climbed down through
the chimneys to leave the children's presents in their stockings for
them to discover and unwrap on Christmas morning. And on
Christmas Day, families sat around the table eating a huge stuffed
turkey, Brussels sprouts and a Christmas pudding, and the Queen
spoke to the nation on the television screen. This was the British
Protestant Christmas. The Queen appeared in a simple but smart
pastel green dress, a triple row of pearls around her neck and a
diamond brooch on her lapel, sitting at her desk surrounded by

photographs of her family and looking straight ahead at her subjects who watched her in their living rooms.

'. . . Reconciliation is the product of reason, tolerance and love, and I think that Christmas is a good time to reflect on it. It is not something easy to achieve, but things that are worth while seldom are . . . A few weeks ago I met in my home a group of people who are working for better understanding between people of different colours, different faiths and different philosophies, and who are trying to solve the very real problems of community relations,' she said in the same year that a particular Member of Parliament was demanding amid popular support that 'aliens' should be encouraged, or maybe persuaded, with the offer of '£1000 per head', to go home. He pointed out that one million repatriations in five years at even double that price would produce hardly a ripple on the surface of then recent budgets.

'Home?'

Ruth wondered, if the hypothetical situation be considered in which 'repatriation' became law, where in her case would she be sent?

'Auschwitz,' an English friend pointed out . . . but the question didn't arise at that moment in history.

Ruth was getting old. Her mother died, and her children grew up and left home. Every Christmas Eve they had a family reunion and Ruth brought a tree home and carefully attached to its branches the old decorations which her children had enjoyed when they were little, and everybody's presents were placed under the tree. They all sat together around the tree in the lowered lighting of the living room and watched the candles glowing and the sparkle of the baubles and gold and silver tinsel. The white tipped branches of the tree made it look as though it had been in a fresh snowfall.

But on this particular Christmas, her children were away and her husband had gone to America to visit a sick relative. Ruth sat alone in her living room. It was peaceful. She was thinking that this was her first Christmas Eve without a tree since that day in Mexico when she caught sight of her first Christmas tree through the keyhole of the bathroom door, reflected on the mirror in the hallway. She was contemplating the diversity of the experiences she had lived through, and how she had been rather like a piece of pasta dough that is squeezed through the pasta machine into a shape while the settings keep getting switched, to emerge on the other side in a jumbled muddle. So she had been subjected to one particular set of cultural forces after another after another . . . ending up in a confused mixture of identities. But she was beginning to understand that she simply was the sum of all those experiences and memories, each of which had made its own enriching contribution towards the person she had become. After all, the mind is more pliant than pasta dough! Yes, she had been curious and puzzled by all the different ways of life, customs, viewpoints and ideas she had encountered and she had often wondered: where in that plan did she fit in? She had tried to absorb and adjust to various ways. But now, as she watched the light from the street lamp flickering through the branches of the tree which were quietly swaying in front of the living room window in that pitch-dark wintry night, she realized that she was all her experiences rolled into one, and she felt at peace with herself. She didn't feel the need any more to *belong* to any particular group: to do so, she understood, inevitably aligned her *against* other groups, which in turn would perpetuate the vicious circle of which she herself had been a victim, the vicious circle which had determined her own dispossession, and the pain and death of countless others. She was at the same time her own unique combination of life events which made her different, and at one with all of mankind. She felt, at that moment, a common bond with every human being, even those who hardened and cut themselves off, surely if it were possible to chip away at their thick layer of ice, there was a chance that in some deep, forgotten recess inside them one might find laughter, pain, fear, care and love . . .

She was sitting quietly in the soft lighting of her living room on that Christmas Eve, and she now saw through the window the brilliant disc of the moon rising behind the tree. The black, slender branches barely moved in the breeze, while feathery clusters of coppery pink clouds slowly sailed by in a sky which had turned a deep translucent blue. She thought of the snow-capped peaks of mountains which she had once seen capturing the first rosy glints of the sun at dawn, and she remembered the chirruping of birds which she had heard coming out of the silence before the night is through, the small wild violet, yellow, pink and blue flowers in the fields, the glassy surface of a lake on a warm, windless day. And she understood that she was all that too.

the cloven hoof

francis king

'Darling, I feel so *bad* about leaving you over Christmas,' Mummy exclaimed yet again, as Laura said goodbye to her and Daddy at the airport before they flew off to Naples to board their ship. 'I shouldn't have dreamed of going away if my arthritis hadn't given me such hell all this month. But you'll have lots of friends to see, won't you?'

'And you can always go to Aunt Iris,' Daddy said.

'Or the Cudlipps.'

Daddy told Laura to drive home very, very slowly. He was thinking at least as much of the BMW as of her.

'Oh, and pet, you will take the greatest care of my poor little Poochie, won't you? You must now think of yourself as his second mother.' The poodle was scratching himself with an air of rapturous concentration on the end of a rhinestone-studded lead, which Laura was holding in the hand not holding Mummy's crocodile-leather make-up box. Laura nodded and Mummy went on: 'Don't, dear, please don't let him do his business, big or small, on the lawn. Daddy would be awfully peeved if, after that reseeding, he were to come back to find it covered in those horrid orange patches once again. I know it's a nuisance to have to rush home in your lunch hour but I'm afraid there's nothing else for it, is there?' Again Laura nodded. 'And bones, dear – bones. You will remember what bones do to his tum?' Laura said that of course, yes, she would remember what bones did to his tum.

When at last they had vanished from sight into the departure lounge, Laura felt none of the relief that she had promised herself. Poochie might caper about at the end of the jewelled lead, even attempting to cock a leg against some luggage abandoned in his path; she herself felt so far from capering about that she had to force herself not to cry.

'There's that yappy little dog,' their neighbour Mr Purdy boomed good-naturedly at her when, on her return, they came face to face – his flushed and hers wan – in the hall of the mansion flats overlooking Regent's Park. Mummy called him 'a vulgar little man', though in fact he was enormous. Daddy merely returned his greetings with a nod ever since that time when a male guest at one of his all-night parties had used the garden, *their* garden, as not even Poochie was allowed to use it, leaning over the balcony for this purpose.

But Laura had secretly admired and envied Mr Purdy for a long, long time. Certainly he was at least fifty and therefore some fifteen years older than herself; and no less certainly he was grossly overweight, ungainly and often drunk. But there was something jolly, amiable and, yes, even sexy about him; so that it was not really surprising that a succession of young girls should have taken up residence with him, albeit each for no more than a week or even a weekend at a time.

Laura smiled at him and then halted – both things she would not have done if Mummy and Daddy had been at hand.

'I thought you'd gone away for Christmas,' he said, and then belched audibly behind a pudgy fist. 'I saw you loading up the BMW. With all those suitcases I guessed that you might all be emigrating.'

Laura explained that Mummy and Daddy had left on a three-week Mediterranean cruise, but that she herself had been unable to go too because of her work.

'And what *do* you do? I've often wondered.'

'I'm at the Foreign Office.'

'How very glamorous!'

Laura did not explain that to be Sir Andrew's secretary was far from being glamorous. Instead, she looked down at Poochie, whimpering for his dinner at the end of his lead, with a shy, furtive smile.

'Well, you must come in for a drink some time. Especially as you're now enjoying your freedom.'

'I'd love that. I'm – I'm told that you have some really lovely things.'

'Good God! Who told you that?'

'Mr Roberts.'

Mr Roberts, the porter, enjoyed gossiping to the residents about each other.

'He must be off his nut.'

The days dragged by and Christmas crept nearer and nearer; but the invitation for which Laura continued to wait with so much eagerness never materialized. She glimpsed Mr Purdy from time to time. Indeed, she herself more than once precipitated an encounter, lurking behind the net curtains of the sitting room until she saw him approach the block and then running out. But though he boomed 'Hello there!' or 'Beastly weather!' in the friendliest fashion, he never said anything further.

Laura blamed the French girl, so often now to be seen swinging from his arm, her triangular, kittenish face upturned to his square, bovine one.

There had been a terrible night when Laura had been woken by thumps and bangs, as of furniture being overturned, and the crash and clatter of breaking crockery, all interspersed with shrill cries and deep bellowings in a mixture of English and French. ''elp! 'elp!' she had heard at one moment; but, cowering under the bedclothes, she did not think of either offering or summoning 'elp.

The next day Laura saw Mr Purdy dragging himself heavily up the steps, a bag from the off-licence round the corner dangling from either swollen hand. There was a piece of sticking plaster puckered across the bridge of his nose, and an aubergine-coloured bruise darkened one side of his dimpled chin.

Laura hurried out into the hall, pulling on her overcoat for appearances. 'Have you had an accident?' she asked disingenuously.

'You might call it that.'

'A fall?'

'A fall? Yes, you might call it that too. One tends to return to reality with a nasty thump.' He hunted in his distended pocket for his keys. 'What a Christmas! And on top of it all my job has folded up.'

Laura had long since learned from Mr Roberts that Mr Purdy wrote a weekly column on dining out for a newspaper which Daddy and Mummy would never have dreamed of having delivered to their flat. In consequence she bought it every Thursday to read in her lunch hour.

'You've been made redundant!'

'If you want to use that euphemism. I'd prefer to say that I've had the boot.'

'Oh, I *am* sorry! I love your pieces. You make one feel that one's actually eaten all those meals.'

'Yes, food *is* interesting. And satisfying. I sometimes think that there's really nothing quite so interesting and satisfying in the whole world. Even better than a good . . .' He broke off with a guffaw. 'Come in and have that drink I promised!' He indicated the upstairs with a jab of the keys in his hand.

Laura, who had for so long been looking forward to this moment, now felt an overwhelming panic. He was all too clearly drunk; and last night she had heard him roaring 'Slut! Slut! Slut!' at that French girl, after which there had been the sound of a slap and a scream of piercing shrillness. No, she could not face it, not all alone. So, quickly, nervously, she said that she was sorry but she was just going out to do some last-minute Christmas shopping.

'To hell with Christmas!'

Laura, scurrying to St John's Wood High Street, cursed herself for having been such a coward.

But the next evening, returning late from work, she was bolder. Glimpsing Mr Purdy as he was about to march into the pub at the corner of their street, she slipped in behind him. 'The usual,' he was saying. Then, catching sight of her, 'Hell*o*, my pet! Never seen you here before. You *are* getting bold. What can I order for you?' It was obvious that the double whiskey being set down before him was not his first of the day.

But Laura, who had always had such a fastidious horror of drunkenness and drunks, now strangely did not care. Indeed, all the symptoms of his condition – the slurring of the speech, the heaviness of the eyelids, the loud and unfocused *bonhomie* – in some way had even started to excite her.

They sat down in a corner and soon he was telling her how at first he had thought her a God-awful toffee-nosed little bitch but now he realized that he just couldn't have been more wrong. It must be those parents of hers. For Christ's sake, what had she done to deserve such parents? In other circumstances Laura would have leapt to their defence; but, like all the other symptoms of his drunkenness, this rudeness about Daddy and Mummy now only gave a sharper edge to her excitement.

Then he began to talk about Christmas: how he always loathed it and how this year he was going to loathe it even more than usual, now that that little tramp had walked out on him and that Old Etonian shit had grabbed his job; how he had a good mind to get pissed and retire to bed until the whole bloody pantomime was over; how turkey and plum pudding and mince pies always made him want to puke . . .

It was then – the excitement surging up within her, an irresistible tide – that Laura swallowed hard, cleared her throat and came up with her invitation: 'I'll also be on my own. So why don't we both . . .?'

Mummy, who was a good, plain cook, had never allowed Laura to do anything in the kitchen other than wash up, prepare the vegetables and scrub the floor when the Portuguese 'treasure' was away – as she was now. But, having committed herself to a Christmas dinner, Laura now realized that she would have to search through

Mummy's cookery books for a dish both elaborate enough to please an expert ('Not, for Christ's sake, *not* a bird!' he had admonished) and simple enough for her to produce with success. After reading cookery books through almost a whole night, she eventually decided – seduced chiefly by the instruction 'Preparation for this dish to begin 3–4 days before it is required' – on a *Boeuf estouffade d'Avignon*.

The next day (since only four days now intervened till Christmas) there was a long quest during her lunch hour for the sprig of rosemary required for the marinade and an equally long contemplation of Daddy's wine racks before selecting the claret to be used for the same purpose. The day after that, again in her lunch hour (Sir Andrew scolded her for her lateness in returning) she went in search of some pickled pork, arrowroot and coriander seeds. On Christmas Eve she reread the recipe and realized, to her horror, that she had omitted to procure a pig's trotter and had no idea where to find one. It was only after she had trailed the whole length of the North End Road, on the advice of a colleague who lived in Fulham, that she at last tracked one down.

Everything was now ready. The three pounds of filet steak had been marinated; she had even practised, the previous evening, making some of the pastry with which the recipe said that the lid of the casserole must be sealed. Again she had read the final instructions: 'The cooking, which must be very, very slow – the slowness can hardly be overemphasized – should, for best results, take 6–7 hours . . .' She had set her alarm clock for six on Christmas morning.

'What a marvellous smell!' Mr Purdy – who had asked her to call him Willy in the pub – exclaimed, as he marched into the flat, a bottle of Lafite Rothschild in either hand and a Camembert cheese tucked precariously under an arm.

'I hope it'll be all right. It's the first time I've attempted this particular dish.'

'What is it?'

She told him and he whistled. 'Thank God it's not a bloody bird.

I can see this is going to be a real gastronomic adventure, Laura my dear.'

Each time that Laura tried to lure him into the dining room he insisted on yet another glass of Daddy's Manzanilla Pasada; but at last, when it was almost four o'clock, there he was slouched at the other end of the table, in excited if groggy anticipation, his napkin tucked into his overtight collar, and there she was, saying nervously, 'I didn't prepare anything for starters,' as she carried in the French earthenware casserole.

'Christ – what an odour! One can't call it a smell. Laura, my sweet – I can see that you know your way to a man's heart. A Cordon Bleu cook – like my late but not otherwise lamented wife!'

Laura cracked the pastry round the lid, baked to the consistency of clay in a drought; and then, with a palpitating heart, she raised the lid itself.

What looked like a sediment of semi-liquid mud was caked at the bottom and on the sides of the casserole. Embedded in it, bleached and bare, was a single cloven hoof: all that was left of the pig's trotter.

'Christ!'

'What's happened to it? What's *happened*?'

'The pastry couldn't have sealed the lid. Evaporation, my dear. Or maybe the oven . . . Perhaps you left it in too long.'

For a few seconds Laura was frozen in horror. Then she snatched up the casserole, burning the ball of her thumb as she did so, rushed into the kitchen and clattered it down into the sink. Oh, hell, hell! It was his fault for having drunk on and on and on; and it was her fault for not having given him a shove. With furious, stricken eyes she stared out into the garden, where Poochie was straining at his business in the middle of the lawn.

She flung up the window. 'Poochie!'

Terrified by her tone, he cringed over to her.

'There you are! Take that! See what that does to your tum!' She picked the pig's trotter out of the casserole and hurled it not so much to him as at him. Now not merely the ball of her thumb but all the tips of her fingers were burning.

Slowly she went back into the dining room, feeling her fingertips still burning, burning, burning and tears pricking at her eyes.

Mr Purdy – Willy – was guzzling a biscuit piled high with the Camembert he had brought. 'Not to worry,' he told her airily, waving the remainder of the biscuit back and forth before his face. 'This claret is first rate. And this Camembert has achieved just the right degree of ripeness. Here. Have some. A real treat.'

Mechanically she cut herself a sliver of Camembert, took a biscuit from the barrel, and then placed the first on top of the second.

She bit into the biscuit. The dry crumbs filled her mouth; but somehow she could not swallow them. It was as if all the dust of her thirty-four years with Daddy and Mummy had suddenly exploded behind her teeth and in the back of her throat, to suffocate her.

'Have a sip of this, old girl.'

He held out, not her glass, but his own, the claret glinting in it.

She shook her head, her mouth still parched with biscuit and the tears still pricking at her eyes.

'Try some. It's a cure for all disappointments. None better. Go on.'

Slowly she put her lips forward to the glass he was uptilting to her. She gulped and gulped again; and then suddenly, miraculously, the dust had gone.

She smiled across at him.

'See? What did I tell you?'

He put a swollen, purplish hand over her bony, pallid one. Then he splashed some more wine into his glass and once again held it up to her lips.

This time she drained it greedily.

white peacocks

sheena joughin

Eileen Cley was watching television, with a bowl of soup balanced on her knees. She had been cooking soup as a film had begun, about half an hour before, and was not sure what was happening, but was enjoying the rhythm of the screen. It was a black and white film in Russian, which did not entirely fill the square of her set, but stretched in a band across its centre. Above and below the slow-moving story were two grey slices of fallow glass. Long and pleasing shapes, with curving edges. The film had subtitles, but these were not often necessary since nothing much was said. Two bulky men in woollen hats and high-laced boots were sitting opposite each other at a table in a small dark room. They were drinking from tiny glasses, which one of them refilled often from a bottle wrapped in straw. They drank and spat and coughed and smoked, and nodded their wide faces. Suddenly there was a stream of speech, and then a line of print at the bottom of the picture.

Yassoff has peacocks, it said.

Eileen licked the back of her spoon then wiped the rim of her bowl with a finger and licked that too. Then she bent from her sagging armchair to drop the bowl to the floor for her dog to lick.

'Yassoff has peacocks, Bruno,' she told him, as he lumbered over. He dipped his long head into the willow patterned porcelain and Eileen fingered his thick limp ears. Soft wads of warmth. Floppy, like the red fox fur her mother used to wear. Bruno was a red setter.

On the television the men were moving. Scraping their benches back and saying something as they stood.

Come and see her, Eileen read, and the camera pulled back to watch the two of them amble across the low-beamed room to a narrow planked door at the back of the set. The taller of them stooped to shoulder his way into a smaller, darker place. This was a bedroom, with a deep-set window and an iron-framed bed. There was a rumpled quilt on the bed which lumped up in its centre, and a pale elbow making an angle on the bolster at the top. The camera traced the shape of the elbow then moved to find a narrow white hand hanging limp towards the stone flagged floor. Someone was asleep, or dead perhaps.

Bruno rolled over and thudded down in front of the two-bar electric fire that Eileen used to heat herself at night.

'Yassoff has peacocks, Bruno,' she told him. 'Don't go to sleep yet,' and she reached out her bare foot to pull at the hair of his tummy with her curled-up toes. He opened his eyes then closed them again. From the television came a scraping sound of the bedroom door being shut.

The thinner man had taken off his hat and was rubbing his head. Eileen assumed he was visiting since he was wearing a coat hunched into a wide leather belt, and looked generally more restless than the other. He was talking now, looking at the door he had just backed out of. *My wife was the same when her mother died. She did not eat. The fire was cold for three weeks. I worked every day and in the evening it was always the same. I went to Yassoff. He gave me a peacock. Maria was better. Our son was born.*

The subtitles stopped, but the speech went on. The bottle was passed. The guest tightened his belt. More print appeared on its thin black tape: *Yassoff has peacocks now, again. White peacocks. You must make a run, my friend.*

'White peacocks, Bruno,' said Eileen, and pulled her knees up, to rub the joints. It was raining and the damp made her stiff. 'White peacocks. Are there such birds, I wonder.'

Bruno shifted his weight and knocked the wire which connected the television aerial to the back of the set. It fell backwards, from its pile of paperbacks, and into a branch of pine tree that Eileen had tacked on to the floral wallpaper earlier that night. The picture on the screen fuzzed. Eileen unfolded herself, wincing slightly as her back straightened out, and moved to free the aerial from her token Christmas tree. The branch was sparse, and dropping its needles already, into the warm slits at the back of the television set.

Someone had given it to Eileen as she'd been walking through the market, earlier that day.

'Here, lovely. Stick the presents round this,' the man with the tinsel on his head had said, as he pressed it into her coat. 'And you can have a box of beetroot, too, for half a quid, seeing as how it's Christmas.'

Eileen always liked the market on late Saturday afternoons in winter. She liked the light-bulb strings shining white on to cauliflower heads and the tangerines, half-wrapped in their lit-up tissue paper. She liked the stallholders drinking cans of beer behind their little altars. The skinned rabbits and the chickens hanging upside down. There were turkeys today, of course, glowing eerie white and wrinkled. With loose necks, like old ladies. She looked at her hands as she set the aerial down again. Her wedding ring was too big; the skin at her wrist was slack. Bracelets, her mother had called those creases, when Elizabeth had been a plump-armed baby. But these were different marks. 'Old hands,' she thought, and rubbed them together. She put them down for Bruno to lick.

'Yes, you liked the market, didn't you, old Bruney? All that buying and selling and rubbish. I expect that woman in bed would cheer up if they took her to the market once in a while. She might like a box of beetroot. What do you think, Bruno?' Eileen laughed to herself as the dog slumped in front of the stove again. He was old now too. They'd bought him for Elizabeth's thirteenth birthday, and that must have been fifteen years ago, at least.

Of course Steven had said the house was too small for a dog. Everything was always too small for Steve. Everything except

Elizabeth, who was perfect, naturally. Perhaps Steve had been just too tall. Certainly Eileen's mother had thought so.

'Why do you live with that bad-tempered lamp post?' she used to say. More often as she got more bad-tempered and smaller herself. And then Elizabeth had grown so tall too, as if to spite her. 'Daughters shouldn't outgrow their mothers.' As if Eileen could do something about it. She couldn't stop Elizabeth doing anything, so she could hardly have told her to not grow any more.

Eileen hadn't seen her daughter for a long time. She'd left a few weeks after Steve's accident. She wondered if she'd grown at all since. Imagine if she'd never stopped growing. She'd be a giant by now. No wonder she lived in Ireland. She could stand at the side of the Giant's Causeway and hitchhike all day long.

On the television the man with the bedridden wife was hammering posts into the ground in falling snow. He must be making his chicken run. Eileen's mother had kept chickens. She had had to pluck one once and had never been able to eat chicken since. Nor turkey either. She would be having fish at her sister's, tomorrow. She always went over there on Christmas Day. They talked about the past, which changed every year, and they went for a walk.

'Would you like a walk, Bruno, my love?' she asked the sleeping mound at her feet. 'I don't know if we'll see these peacocks at all.'

There were two men in blanket coats on her screen. They were in the cab of a smoky van, with dance music crackling from a radio. One of them spoke, and Eileen read: *We must walk soon. The snow is extra deep.*

'Extra deep?' said Eileen, 'only children say "extra deep". I'll have a cup of tea, Bruno, then we'll have a little walk, and then I think it really will be bedtime.'

She made her way along a narrow papered corridor to the back of the house, wondering how long it had been since someone had told her to go to bed. You had to go to bed early on Christmas Eve, of course, or Father Christmas wouldn't come. The kitchen had a flat roof, which echoed the sound of the rain outside. A bus splashed to a stop across the road. There were footsteps and a man's voice, shouting.

'No, not here. Come on. There's one open under their flat. We'll get some cans in there.'

A party. A Christmas party with mistletoe and glitter and drinking. She plugged in the kettle. Perhaps the woman in the film would get up for a party. She might enjoy dressing up, even though her mother was dead. Perhaps more so, in fact. Eileen used to like parties. She had once worn a peacock feather in a hat to a fancy dress affair, she remembered. Steven had gone as the Devil. So had four other men, which had annoyed him, although he was the tallest, of course. Eileen couldn't remember where she'd got the feather. She ate half a digestive biscuit whilst the kettle boiled. White peacocks.

She'd never heard of them. She must ask her sister. The kettle bubbled and spilled itself into a bowl of caster sugar. Eileen switched it off at the wall and there was silence in the rainy house. She listened for a moment. She listened as if something was about to happen. As if there were a child, asleep upstairs, or an animal, lost outside. The doorbell rang. The doorbell rang and Bruno barked and lolloped down the hallway. Eileen sat down on a chair which she had left in the middle of the room when she'd been replacing a light bulb the day before. Bruno came galloping into her, barking and nosing her legs. She looked at the clock, which was sometimes right, and it said eleven thirty-five. The bell rang again.

Eileen stood and walked along the passageway with its crumbling floral mouldings and its smell of dog, and she took an old raincoat down from a tilted coatrack to her left. She buttoned herself up and smoothed her strong hair back into her wide red Alice band. She took Bruno's lead from its peg. If it was someone she didn't want to see, she would say she was on her way out. She wasn't expecting anyone. She held Bruno's collar and opened the door.

'Mrs Cley?' Someone tall was framed in her arched porchway, silhouetted by an orange street lamp. 'Are you Lizzie's mother? I'm a friend of hers, from Galway.'

The man's voice swayed up and down, in a singing Irish accent.

Eileen nodded and stared at him. He was stooping slightly, behind a bulky rucksack, and at her eye level was a long slim hand, with ringed fingers, curved around something strapped to his front. Two white woollen threads of legs were dangling from it.

'Is that a baby?' She moved back slightly.

'Yes, it's mine. Could I come in?'

Eileen looked at Bruno, who was looking at her, then she looked into the young man's face again. He had something shiny in the flesh of his nose. He had a high forehead, and a mass of tangled hair. He smiled a wide soft smile. Eileen stepped back into her hallway.

'All right,' she said, 'come in.' There was a twisted smell of woodsmoke as he bent to lift his bag and brushed past to stand tall, at her side.

'It's on the left,' she said. 'I was just making a pot of tea.'

She turned and followed her visitor into the sitting room, where two men were embracing, on the television set. Like bears, Eileen thought. Like hills with hands.

'It's a film about peacocks, I think,' she said, 'although I was making soup when it started.'

'I'm Louis,' said her guest, and stretched out his hand, which was cold and held hers tightly, with its thumb reaching up above her wrist. He seemed colossal in Eileen's room, with his glints of silver and gold-ringed ears. Like a tree in her house with his green felt jacket and velvet legs. His jacket was embroidered with woollen flowers and buttoned up to the neck with square brass buttons. His hair was long and strands of it were wrapped in coloured threads, falling on to the bundle at his front.

Eileen moved nearer to him and tiptoed to see the baby's face. It was pale with freckles and high arched brows.

'What an angel,' she said, putting a finger to its knuckled nose. 'Would it be happier lying flat?' She straightened a cushion on the couch against the wall.

'It seems very small to be alone,' she said. 'What is it called?'

'Oonagh,' said Louis, and stroked the soft white hair at the top of his bound-up bundle. He reached behind his back and unstrapped the sling. He rolled Oonagh over into the crook of his arm and bent to blow gently on to her curled-up fingers.

'Yes she's very small.' He smiled as he lowered her on to the couch. 'She's four months old today. But she's not alone, she's with me. I've brought her to see my granny, for Christmas.' He stretched, arching his back, then leaned forward to touch his toes.

'I've walked miles with her today.' He smiled up at Eileen, more surely this time. 'I look after Oonie a lot of the time anyway. Cascade works most nights. She works with Lizzie in fact. They run a sort of hostel place for down and outs in Galway. Lizzie's great with Oonagh too. She was there when she was born. Cass had her at home. We share a cottage over there.'

'So you live with my daughter?'

'No. I live with Cascade. She's Oonagh's mother, you see. Lizzie lives with Joey, but we share a cottage. Well, two cottages really.' He laughed.

'Look I'm sorry we just arrived in on you like this. I thought I had a phone number but I couldn't find it, so I wasn't sure what to do. That was the only train I could get.' He rubbed his forehead with both his hands. 'I only decided to come last night and Lizzie said you mightn't mind me waiting around here till we could see Gran. She's in a home off the Holloway Road. It won't be open until tomorrow morning.'

Eileen watched the baby's hands as they curled a little tighter around the air above its tummy.

'I'm surprised Elizabeth still knows my address,' she said, and bit on the side of her mouth. 'She hasn't spoken to me for six years.'

'She looks like you,' said Louis. He knelt down to his bag which was patchworked with huddled runs of blanket stitch. It had brass buckles, like an old trunk of Steve's that was still in the attic, she remembered suddenly. Full of Elizabeth's stuff.

'Liz gave me something for you. I hope it's still in here.'

Louis began to unravel his bag. He pulled at bits of paisley and a Fair-Isle sweater. A yellow wallet slipped to the floor, then some disposable nappies, and a length of blue glass beads. A brick of fruit and nut chocolate slid into the gap between his crimson legs and he passed it over on to Eileen's knees. A bottle of whiskey knocked against the buckles of the bag as he rolled it free. He unscrewed the top.

'Do you mind if I have a drink?'

Eileen shook her head. She watched as the amber splashed up into the neck of the bottle then down again as he took a mouthful. He wiped his mouth with the back of his hand. He held it out towards her. She smiled.

'I think I'll have some in a glass, thanks.'

'I'll find you one if you tell me where to look.' Louis unbuttoned his jacket, and pulled it back and off. He was wearing a woven shirt with red panels in its yoke. Eileen realized she was still wearing her raincoat and stood to undo it as she directed Louis to the cupboard on the wall above the pine branch. She noticed that the bedridden woman was sitting up, on the television set. She was being passed a steaming bowl by a man in a coat. *I am so hungry* flashed up on to her wrinkled quilt. Then Louis's legs cut the picture in half as he reached behind the set, for glasses.

Eileen thought how nice it was to watch someone getting something out of a cupboard. She watched Louis wipe two tumblers clean with the hem of his shirt. He half-filled one and passed it to Eileen. She leaned back into her chair and pulled her legs up into her cashmere breast and felt like a guest herself.

'How nice,' she said. She looked at the baby. Oonagh whimpered softly.

'It must be nearly time for her bottle,' Louis decided, and stooped over his daughter to lift her up on to his shoulder. She looked as if she'd been blown there, Eileen thought. Like a leaf that had caught in the web of his hair.

'Shall I hold her for you, while you find everything?'

'Thanks,' and Eileen felt the sudden lightness of a baby on her lap. She put her little finger into its mouth and felt the strength of its sucking tongue. Louis knelt down to his rucksack again. He took a swig from the bottle he'd left on the tapestry carpeted floor and pulled out a pair of crumpled corduroy trousers.

'I thought I'd bring something respectable to wear to see Gran,' he explained as he laid them across the floor. 'She hasn't seen me for three years. She doesn't even know I'm a father yet.' Eileen thought how pleasant it was to hold a baby and drink whiskey at the same time.

'I haven't done it for years,' she said. Then, 'How old is your grandmother?'

'She'll be ninety this year. She'll love Oonagh. She loves baby girls. When I was a kid she'd make frocks for the whole street, and then some. She used to live with us.' Louis took another gulp from the bottle at his side.

'She's called Oonagh too. So was my mum.'

He held the top of his rucksack up with one hand and pushed the other deep inside it. He pulled out a small flat packet, wrapped in tissue paper. 'From Lizzie. Happy Christmas Mrs Cley.' He rested the present on top of the baby, on her knee.

'Does Elizabeth talk about me much?'

Louis was sucking the teat of a baby's bottle. He wiped it with the palm of his hand, then licked it clean again.

'Liz is not a great talker, Mrs Cley.'

'I suppose not,' said Eileen, remembering silent teatimes and the front door slamming. 'She used to like singing.'

'Oh yes, she sings all right,' said Louis. 'She plays a mean bass guitar as well. You can be proud of that girl Mrs Cley. She'll go far.'

Eileen thought that Elizabeth had gone far enough for her. She sat curled around Oonagh and opened her present as she listened to Louis moving around in the kitchen. He was humming to himself and opening and closing drawers. Someone in the next room. That's what her mother had told her marriage would be. A consolation. This was her consolation prize then; an oval wooden hair clasp. It was pale and roughly carved and there was a folded note around it which said 'I made this for you. Elizabeth.' The handwriting was full of loops, like her knitting used to be. It was hard teaching children to knit, Eileen remembered. She pulled softly at Oonagh's plump little fingers. She tried to imagine them holding knitting needles.

Now it's nearly one o'clock and the whiskey bottle is almost empty. It's still raining heavily and occasionally the blocked guttering outside overspills. On the television set the woman whose mother has died is sitting in a basket chair, rocking slightly and moving her lips. Singing something. Bruno is drinking warm water from the bowl that Louis heated the bottle in, and Oonagh is asleep on the armchair. Eileen is sitting on the floor with her hair coiled up into her new carved clasp. She's talking about being lonely, which she's never done before. She's telling Louis about her mother. How she remembers her on the top landing, one night, shortly before she died.

'She was there in her nightie with her stick in the air, staring up at the ceiling. It was Elizabeth who called me. She'd woken up with a nightmare and been coming into our bed, like she always did, and she'd walked into my mother with her stick. She was terrified. She thought it was a ghost. I went out and Elizabeth was crying and my mother was just standing there, staring into space. I went to mother and I took her hand and I asked her if there was anything she wanted. She just stared. She stared at me for ages and then eventually she let go of my hand and started wandering back into her room. She stopped for a moment though. She looked back at me, and she said, very clearly, "I want my mother, but she's dead." Then she went back to bed. I think I felt more lonely then than I ever have again.'

Louis rubs his face in his hands then smooths his hair away over his shoulders and stretches his legs. 'The sea made me lonely today,' he says, 'it was so big and flat and black. And Oonagh makes me feel lonely, sometimes, when she cries for no reason. I suppose I miss my mother then.' Eileen nods and watches her whiskey as she tilts it back and forth.

'Shall I make up a bed for the baby?' she says. 'I'd like to do that. We could put her in a drawer.'

Louis is folding a rug around Oonagh. She's tucked into a mahogany drawer from the chest in Eileen's bedroom. They emptied it together and there is now a hill of sliding clothes at the foot of her unmade bed. A bottle of eau de Cologne had been spilled in the process. Louis said it was his favourite smell. It is Eileen's too. Oonagh is asleep and Louis is sitting beside her makeshift cot, holding his knees and looking at Eileen.

'You don't look so much like Lizzie with your hair up on your head like that. You've got a longer face. And a different mouth.'

'We had different fathers,' says Eileen. She laughs and watches Louis's neck stretch back as he drains the last of his glass. She thinks how nice he is to look at, bundled into himself, like a child. She doesn't want to go to bed. He won't be here tomorrow night. There will be no one to tell about her Christmas Day. She'd like to bring him home some cake. She'd like to kiss him good-night. She supposes she won't. She stands up and goes to the door. She puts out her hand to the handle, then stops and turns and takes the clasp out of her hair. She's going to say good-night.

'You could sleep in my bed, if you'd like to,' she says, instead, and suddenly wishes he would. She wishes she could be Oonagh instead of herself. It must be lovely, being a baby. Louis looks up at her and grins.

'I think I'd better sit it out down here, with the television set,' he says. 'You're lovely, Mrs Cley.' And Eileen leaves the room.

Now the film is drawing to a close. A woman in a stranded shawl is scattering handfuls of grain into a chicken-wire enclosure, and a child in a cape and knee-length boots is running across the screen. He is pointing, shouting something. *Look. On the tree*, the subtitle says. The camera pans, and there in the branches of a leafless tree, beyond a parked tractor and a bonfire, is the huddled white shape of a bird, at rest. A violin starts to play. The child is running to its mother, shouting. *Can peacocks fly, Mama? Can peacocks fly?* 'Of course they can,' says Louis, as he switches the television off.

'Anything can fly.'

At the top of the stairs, at the banisters' end, is an embroidered jacket, hanging. On the floorboards outside Eileen Cley's door is a pile of folded clothes. On the bed the mattress dips as Louis moves under the quilt. On the pillow an elbow is unbent as Eileen reaches out to touch a lock of cedar-smelling hair.

'Christmas,' says Louis, as he takes her hand.

'Christmas Day,' she says, as she curls into sleep, wrapped into the warmth of his long and very white shape.

the hand of god

seán mac mathúna

Doyle – No. 12 in class 6B, refectory table No. 4, cubicle No. 7 in
St. Brendan's dormitory, altar boy No. 17, No. 3 in Computer Club
– was being disgraced.

For five years they had tolerated his promoting the cause of communism. It was not a philosophy with him, rather a chemistry,
because pushing communism demanded emotional reserves. Fr.
Healy would have said more of a sickness. Five years ago he had
recommended that Doyle be expelled, but it was pointed out to him
that those days had gone.

Doyle had remained at school with what he called his gods, Mao,
Castro, Connolly, Che Guevara, Lenin, Jim Larkin, to fight the
valiant fight against the reactionary bourgeois forces. These were
almost everybody from The Red Cross to 'The International
Conspiracy of Freemasons'. One of his heroes was Rubik, from
Hungary [communist country]. Rubik invented the cubes. Rubik
was a genius. 'With people like Rubik we can't lose,' he said. And in
Doyle's head there was a revolutionary charter for the world that
distinctly said no retribution. Those days were gone he said. Just
some changes. Yes, changes.

Fr. Healy would rather be playing basketball than teaching. Still,
history was OK – if it weren't for Doyle, who had read more history
than Healy, and never missed a chance to show it. And he also knew
more French. One day while Healy was teaching the French
Revolution a pupil asked him why the deputies always met in a hotel,

the Hôtel de Ville. Healy gave it a lot of thought before answering. ''Twas handy for sandwiches, and then there was the bar,' he said.

Doyle had to point out acidly that Hôtel de Ville simply meant Town Hall in French. Healy looked like someone who had been slapped across the mouth. The class looked at Doyle. So did Healy and in that fleeting glance the cross hairs of fate fastened on Doyle's forehead. Doyle had grown in stature and had an extra half dozen added to his following. These were the usual disaffected, deprived, orphaned, rebellious, thick, inspired fringe of humanity who are always on the lookout for a possible champion. To them he distributed free copies of Vladimir Cheboksarov's *The Decline of the Western World* which the CPI sent him regularly.

The other priests knew about Doyle, most of them treating him as a welcome exotic on the bleak landscape of a school timetable. Others didn't. One, the ancient Fr. Crilly, used to mutter to him in the corridor, 'What a pity your mother dropped you on your head, Doyle.' Or, 'I can't for the life of me figure out how a Doyle ever got around to writing Sherlock Holmes.' Fr. Cleary and Fr. Fitzgibbons were two others. 'Doyle,' said Fr. Cleary, 'it isn't as if ye were badly off at home, what with twenty cows, a sand pit, and a small shop with two petrol pumps; in any communist country worth its salt you would all be hanged for exploiting the poor.'

The boy was stung, all the more for its being true. But it was not his nature to bow gracefully. 'Fr. Cleary, do you think that owning a Honda Civic, having an expensive golf membership, a palatial apartment, gourmet meals on tap, and twenty-five grand a year salary makes you Christlike? Not bad for a man that has taken a vow of poverty,' he had flung at the priest and stalked off. Doyle went to the locker rooms where he endlessly told his friends of his most recent victory; but the boy had no friend wise enough to tell him that it can be dangerous to win too often.

Something strange happened to the world that summer of '89, the East began to open its fist. Doyle never noticed it until after the summer holidays when he was asked in class what he thought of Tiananmen Square. '*Agents provocateurs* – they asked for it and they got it!' he had flung back. But the class wouldn't buy that. That's when Healy swooped.

'That's a real pinko answer!' he snapped. There and then Doyle was christened Pinko Doyle. And worse, his followers were called Doyle's Pinkos. The whole shop stigmatized in an instant! He couldn't believe it. Neither could he believe what was happening all over Europe. Healy brought in the newspapers about demonstrations in Frankfurt, and crowds demanding this and that. He revealed what the Stasi were and how secret police propped up other puppet regimes.

At this point Doyle's supporters came in a deputation to him. 'Who are these Stasi?' they asked. 'They are evil, how can they be good communists?'

'Just you wait, you're going to see a miracle,' he winked at them. He would watch the deputation depart though the corridors dragging their shadows after them. But, yes, who were the Stasi?

It was Healy who showed them videos of the Berlin Wall being breached. Night after night Doyle watched these animals savage the wall, while his blood boiled. 'Why are they allowing them to do this?' he asked himself in anguish. Quinlan and O'Meara, his staunchest supporters, came to Doyle in desperation.

'You've got to do something,' they said. 'It's not just the desertions, we are laughing stocks.' Doyle looked at Quinlan, the widow's son from Misk, penniless but brave and bright; at O'Meara, one of a large family on a few acres of mountain, eking out, always eking out.

'I'm going to get that bastard, Healy.'

'It's not Healy, it's the Russians, where are the Russians?'

'It's Healy,' he gritted as he watched them slope away from him. Now he knew the agony of the leader who has led his men into ambush. He raced to his dormitory, threw himself on his bed and stuffed the pillow into his mouth.

In class Healy read excerpts of Havel's plays – real lousy writing, even Doyle could see that – and read out the latest statistics on the true state of the Russian economy, told them of a Catholic church being reconsecrated in the western Ukraine, and then the class turning to Doyle for his view, and Doyle growing more strident, and gamely shouting about plots and conspiracies and all the time the desertions and the going over to Healy. Doyle's gods weren't just jumping off their pedestals, some were doing it off skyscrapers.

If Healy brought down the communist world, it was the Trabant that brought down Doyle. He defended the stinking, noisy, two stroke East German car by attacking the Mercedes, which he called bourgeois scrap. It was at this point that Doyle lost his last supporters. After that his classmates greeted him with spluttery noises and by holding their noses. Healy began to invade Doyle's mind to the extent that the parting between fancy and fact vanished.

At home on Christmas Day while manning the petrol pumps, and hunched against a hailstorm from the west, Doyle heard from a passing cattle dealer that Ceauşescu and his wife had been slaughtered.

'They was raddled be a stengun in the snow,' the man had said. The dealer was towing a trailer of calves, about two months old. Hail hopped off their incipient horns and made their big eyes blink at Doyle. Uncharacteristically he was suddenly overcome with sympathy for the oppressed of this world, and he retired to his room and looked out at the bleak mountainside that was the family farm. Towels of hailstone from the west advanced along the mountain pass brushing its sides with white, backwards and forwards. For seeming ages he watched the approaching squall till finally it swept in upon the house with all its dazzling might, its millions of shot hopping off the corrugated iron roof and rattling the windows, and the more it did the more it illuminated the boy's mind, filling it with a picture of the pair, he, grim and unrelenting, she, hopeful that this charade would be cancelled – till she heard the metal snap of the safety catch, and then the terror in her mind and the rush of words that stuck in her throat as the gun scattered the two of them all over eternity. And Doyle heard the shout of jubilation that echoed round a vengeful world, and it brought a rush of anger to his breast. 'The human race, a gang of bloody foxhounds!' he said as he sat on his bed and choked back the tears.

After Christmas Doyle was left without a friend, for the world of communism had melted away as meekly as an ice-cream. His former colleagues distanced themselves by ridiculing him more than the others. He took to spending most of his time in the dormitory which was against the rules but the priests turned a blind eye. Here as he paced the floor he decided his position was untenable. He would have to leave and do his final exam from home. It was a graceful decision, but Doyle was not graceful.

At night while the rest slept he took to prowling the dark corridors all the way to the east wing; the east wing was forbidden under pain of immediate expulsion. That was fine with him as he was going to expel himself anyway. In the east wing he watched and waited for hours, studying little sounds, spying for lights in windows, eyeing the car park. This went on for a month until Doyle had bags under his eyes from lack of sleep. He was never caught for he had by now become a shadowy figure. But he was excited for he had established a certain correlation between lights or darkness in certain windows and the presence or absence of certain cars in the car park. Doyle had the stopwatch working. 'Gotcha' was all he said as he smiled all the way through the gloom of the senior corridor.

He was elated as he glided silently up the back stairs. He lay back in bed and puffed at a fag end. He couldn't stop chuckling. His eyes became pinpoints as he figured out the best way to humiliate him. There were many ways of doing that but first he had to test the information on somebody.

Next day he collared Quinlan outside the oratory. Quinlan was low sized and had it in for *Homo sapiens* in general whom he saw as mounting a concerted campaign against him. But he didn't want to be seen speaking to Doyle and he backed into the shadows.

'I'm in a hurry,' he snapped as he checked that he wasn't being observed.

'It's a secret for the time being, but I'll tell you, Healy is screwing the new cook,' Doyle said and watched the reaction carefully.

'Really?' Quinlan's eyes widened.

'Yes, this hypocrite, this whited sepulchre, who preaches piety and restraint, is screwing the new cook twice a week, yes, by God, Mondays and Fridays.' It was commonly agreed that the cook had a gorgeous bum that rippled against her starched white housecoat. Doyle could almost feel the image that Quinlan began to weave in his mind but when his pupils began to dilate Doyle knew that the priest was not only envied but admired. They quickly parted and Doyle raced for a lavatory cubicle where he dragged on a butt. He held the smoke as he thought about Quinlan's eyes, the little runt who had never shown any interest in anything except communism, model airplanes and raspberry jam; and if this was his reaction it would be universal among the rest of the college. Revenge! He had to have it.

The following week Doyle went to the nearby cathedral. It wasn't piety that brought him there, more the boredom of alienation. The architect, Pugin, had designed the cathedral in stone. Now the sun designed a second one in shadow and flung it across the lawns. Doyle preferred his cathedrals that way. He strolled up the steps and into the gloom and paused at a pillar in the chancel. It was confession day and the tall pillars and the shadows seemed to encourage little confidences which resulted in bursts of whispering that always reminded Doyle of frying rashers. And to prove that walls couldn't hear they had built them twelve feet thick.

He strolled down the nave and there was the confession box with Healy's name on it; and as he passed he had a sudden insight into the priest's fate. He knelt among a group of old people. He knew they were old for he could smell them. His nostrils twitched and made him raise his eyes up from this unwashed world towards the tumble of buttresses and arches high in the cupola.

Illuminated shafts were stabbing through the tall gloom and the myriads of dust motes that shimmered in them gave the impression of slowly wheeling light. It seemed very high up and distant and in some strange way reminded him of the hailstones last Christmas Day. He could see again the sheets of hail brushing the sides of the mountains before they turned and swept down on the corrugated iron roof with deafening effect. And somewhere in that faraway world also were the snowy bodies of the Ceauşescus. Suddenly he knew precisely what he was going to do.

He got up, took his place in the queue outside the box and when his turn came, in he went. It was pitch dark and the box smelt of woodsmoke the same as the pine desks at the school. Healy yanked the shutter open as if he were on piece-time.

'Bless me, Father, for I have sinned. I'm sleeping with a woman twice a week.'

'Give her up,' the bored voice said.

'I can't, I love her.'

'What would you know about love? What age are you?'

'Seventeen, Father.'

'One way or the other you are too young.'

'Yes, that's what she says too, Father.'

The priest's interest stirred. 'What age is she?'

'I figure about twenty-six or seven.' Doyle felt a weighty body strain closer to him.

'I don't like this at all. What on earth could a woman of that age see in you?'

'A good question, Father. She needs the sex.'

'What makes you think that?'

'Well, Father, I'm sorta handy in bed. Or so they tell me.'

'They?'

'Yes, there have been others. Lots.'

'You'll get Aids!'

'So they tell me. She has a lover her own age but he doesn't, well, I mean he can't, he, how shall I put it?'

'He can't satisfy her?'

'Exactly.'

'This is serious. You'll have to give up this woman, immediately. Get a girl your own age.'

'I can't, Father, I'm in the college.'

'A day boy in the college! This is worse than I thought.'

'No, Father, a boarder!' Doyle felt the breathing getting thicker. They were like two cats straining to see each other in the dark. When he spoke there was exasperation in the tone.

'How on earth could a boarder be having sex with a woman a few nights a week, when he's in the college all the time?'

'That's a fair question, Father, but that's a secret.'

'Nonsense, there can be no secrets in the confessional.'

'Well, in that case, I guess, I can explain. She's the new cook!'

Doyle could already feel the shock in the air and it seemed ages before he heard the frying rashers of absolution. As he came out of the box he was sure of one thing, Healy had not recognized him, for it's difficult to recognize a whisper. That was easily remedied: instead of heading off home he ceremoniously genuflected outside the box and in that instant felt Healy flicking the curtain. That was when he decided that revenge was the sweetest thing in the universe.

After that Doyle had his bags packed – he would go at any moment – except that he was mesmerized by Healy. He found himself watching the man all the more. A few days later he chanced to see him in the company of other teachers in the quad. He was laughing and yarning with them and being ever so charming; and it occurred to Doyle that his little plan for humiliating the priest had failed.

Later that day he was surprised when Quinlan initiated conversation behind the tennis courts. He explained to Doyle that his sister had once told him that most priests have a fling sometime, especially before they were given a parish of their own. And Healy was being given a parish, or hadn't he heard; Misk, admittedly a very poor parish, but it would do for openers. This would end the fling. The second thing he told him was that there wasn't a statue of Stalin standing anywhere in the world except in North Korea. Doyle rushed back to his cubicle, threw himself on his bed and choked tears of anguish back by stuffing the towel down his throat. Whatever about Stalin this vile fornicator who usurped the sacred cloth of Mother Church, and flung the words of Christ back in his teeth, shouldn't be allowed to get away with it. He demanded some form of retribution, like a dressing down by the Abbot or someone. Suddenly it all tumbled beautifully out of somewhere and into his mind. Letters! He would write letters to various people – none of your poison pen stuff, for he would sign his own name. And it was all uncanny, it was as if someone was whispering into his ear.

He went immediately to the computer room and started his first letter to the Head Abbot. It was a rush of eloquence and invective. At one stage he had written, 'and if it is reasonable to send us basketball players to teach history why not rabbits for geography?' Doyle read and reread that sentence till the tears rolled down his face.

He sent one to Monsignor Shorte, scourge of enlightenment, opposer to everything except the rosary, in which he complained of 'a clergy grown indolent and stupid in luxury, who squabbled like schoolboys over privileges, who had neither Latin, restraint, nor the merest whiff of piety! Was it for the likes of Healy that the martyrs had died in the arena?' His style was developing nicely, and he had a turn of phrase that he never knew was in him. And in all the letters he belittled Healy's lack of intelligence. For Doyle's world was going to be run by intelligence and nothing else.

Now he was in his element and he sent six more letters to various clerics until suddenly the memory of Quinlan's eyes dilating brought him up short. These were all men, and if the truth be known, men of the world, they would react the same way, envy and admiration, and they would do nothing about it.

Then one day he saw the Bishop's housekeeper in the orchard scowling from apple to apple. He had once delivered to her a box of Xmas candles at the back door of the palace; she had a Lenten face, one that was eloquent of Fridays, fish, and self-mortification. Bingo! It was that face which inspired him to describe the cook as 'undoubtedly a very pretty woman – although looks aren't everything', and though she had a wonderful female figure 'did she have to flaunt it in the faces of so many adolescent young men while waiting for their dinner?' And it had been recently noted by him and other like-minded students that 'she was smiling a lot'. The housekeeper would become as alert as a cat when she read 'was there any connection between that and dinners that were underdone, as if in some quarters there was an unseemly haste?' She was bound to pounce when he casually asked 'was there after all some foundation to the scandalous rumours that were going around?' He ended the letter with a fervent 'where will it all end, I humbly ask. Yours sincerely, C. Doyle, The Shop, Killawley.'

He was enthralled by the style of his letter to the housekeeper so much that he sent off also a few similar ones to local convents – cut him off at all the passes. Only then did he go home.

The following Christmas Day Doyle was manning the pumps and selling people all the knick-knacks that they had forgotten to lay in; candles, cranberry sauce, pepper, cloves, Milk of Magnesia and rat poison. A great black cloud had built up and was releasing solitary snowflakes that sailed down the pass in single file. Suddenly a Sierra pulled up and out jumped Fr. Healy – in a fawn sports coat with a pair of white Reeboks. Out of the other side hopped a very pretty cook in a navy and whitish get up. Doyle nearly dropped the pump.

'Val, I want you to meet Ciaran Doyle, the man who taught me history,' said Healy putting his arm round her, 'and a little French,' and he winked at the open-mouthed Doyle, 'but not enough for us to have spent our honeymoon in France, so we went to Russia instead. And we bought you a little present, didn't we Val?' Doyle was shocked. Healy had left the church! He looked down at the Donegal tweed, Healy was a turncoat.

'Here,' and he put a bust of Lenin into his hands. 'Now twist off the head, go on, go on,' he chortled. The boy did what he was told, and a smaller Lenin looked up at him. At that moment a snowflake landed on Healy's forehead and promptly melted. The pair on the road squealed with real delight.

'Do it again,' they said. He did. More squeals. God, will this go on for ever, Doyle thought. Seven heads altogether, that's if one were to count the last one which made Lenin look like a leprechaun stuck in a thimble. Was Healy trying to give a little message there? He looked into eyes that hadn't the merest trace of malice.

'Look, Teddy, snow!' Teddy! Doyle wanted to be knocked out.

'Yes, it's because we are so high up. It really is wonderful to be so high up.' He turned to the boy. 'I bet that's why you like history and all that.'

'I don't follow.'

He shrugged, 'Well, the altitude, like.' The man was even more stupid than the boy remembered. 'I never knew much. I used to hate those lessons, and I am deeply sorry, sometimes the Lord gives us more than we can chew. And I wouldn't have made a good priest either, would I, Val?'

'Oh, I don't know about that,' she said coyly, 'you'd have to get a housekeeper, of course.' God if you're there, get rid of these guys fast, but God wasn't there. He thought they were going to start up about the bishop's housekeeper. The weather suddenly decided to put on a show for them and snow began to drift down silently, turning things furry white. Healy stretched out his hands and looking up at the skies said, 'this is, is, ah, this is –'

'Celestial?'

'That's it, celestial.'

'Oh, that's a lovely word, Teddy.' And Doyle had to admit that there was something unusual about the sudden whiteness and, yes, the silence. Up here it's never silent. For a while they said nothing, just watched, and then the two sat in the car, started it up and Healy shouted out of the window. 'It would have been disastrous for me, the end maybe, I am so glad at what happened. Still, I miss it a lot, I haven't turned my back on them. I said before I don't know much academic stuff, but I'm bright enough to see the hand of God. Doyle, it is sad when you don't belong, but not wanting to belong is the cruellest path of all.'

'Yes, and some people are like lost puppy dogs, they can belong anywhere.'

'Goodbye, and thank-you,' he smiled. The Sierra went off down the pass until its purr died in the trees below leaving the boy standing there.

He looked at the petrol pumps, another quick look at this real world of rusting corrugated iron and storm bent white thorns, at the shop which always stank of Jeye's Fluid and firelighters, and he thought especially of its guaranteed lack of event and he knew that this was a good world for puppy dogs. He sighed and went to his room. For a long time he gazed out of the window at a landscape that would now never feel the brunt of his revolution. It would never feel anything but hail to remind the world of vengeance, and now and again some snow to show that there was also forgiveness.

tinsel bright

kirsty gunn

Years before Moma divorced my Dad he used to dress up as a fairy for the hospital every Christmas Day. In that role he was truly beautiful to see. A blond man, and delicately made, he stunned all the patients with his wide variety of fairy outfits, a froth of tulle and sequins, in colours that I would have chosen, if I could have been a fairy too.

This, of course, would never happen. Only doctors were allowed to wear the fairy tutus and the tight spangled bodice with fitted bra. It was the custom at Victoria Grand, the hospital where my father worked as a heart surgeon, for the men to transform themselves this way. For more than fifty years they had tripped the bright wards as elves and pixies on December the 25th, spreading cheer and good humour to even those so ill they couldn't laugh out loud, couldn't leave their beds. It was my Dad's arrival at the hospital however that made the event really special. From his first parade he'd seen the limitations in the green cotton costumes, his red elf tights had chafed him badly and carried the smell of too many wearings.

'As there is no doubt that the annual parade is of enormous benefit to all the patients at Victoria Grand, I would like to suggest we make the event even more entertaining,' he'd announced to the Social Board, quite soon after his first time. 'Therefore, if you'll let me, I'd like to make our parade a Spectacular. I'd like to be in charge of costumes from now on.'

I was perhaps five or six then. I remember it well as being a time of outfits. My new school required that I be dressed in a variety of uniform, pale blue linen dresses for summer, serge pinafores with blue flannel blouses when the months were cool. Moma took me shopping in a special uniform shop and I came home with boxes of blue blazers, coats, hats. There were brown socks and white socks and three different kinds of shoes. Yet, though I loved taking the things from their paper packets, smelling the newness of fabric and leather, none of the clothes pleased me as much, when I put them on, as I hoped. None of them were fairy.

In the mean time, my Dad toiled at the sewing machine, and was planning, planning. What I know now, is that the magic of these Christmases past, in the sparkle of a sequinned bodice, in the stiffened folds of a sugar pink gown, comes from it being a time when doctors were men and men only. Girls didn't dress up and play this game. Even the pretty nurses looked lumpen and unhappy when compared to the sight of senior staff on parade. Giggling, they nudged each other when my Dad darted past them with his tinsel wand. They knew that, with his first Spectacular, 'Fairies from Foreign Lands', he'd started something different. It was only the beginning. 'Fairy Friends of Aladdin' he announced the next year. Then 'Winter Fairies in the Snow. See this trimming, Francie?' He'd lengthen out a piece of bright silver for me to see, but never touch. 'I'm going to stitch it to the hems so it looks like ice . . .'

Still, even though things may have looked like a hospital romance movie, with handsome men treading the wards and a nurse for a woman by their side, my own mother was no sister. She was a painter, just starting out when I was born, but there were big plans for her career, I know. All through the 1960s she was friends with Clement Greenberg and Franz Kline and Helen Frankenthaler, as well as some big gallery dealers in Paris and Berlin. We called her Moma after the gallery in New York City, her favourite place in the whole wide world. I think she liked that. I think it helped her believe things would work out all right for her in the end.

Whatever, it was surely her tenderness with colour that got my Dad falling in love. He'd always wanted to work in the theatre. The heart doctoring was his father's idea, he said, not his, and it had saddened him ever since that he'd let himself be bullied into following a career he didn't care for.

'Don't ever listen to what parents say,' he used to tell me. 'That's my advice. You've got your own life to live and your mother and I don't feature in it, believe me. Follow your instincts, Francie. I wanted costume! Costume! The smell of greasepaint in the air! Now all I have is a Christmas show once a year. I'm a sad man . . .'

Oh, but I didn't believe him. My Dad smiled too much, tickled me too much, to be unhappy. Besides, he'd invented the Victoria Grand Fairy Day, hadn't he? How could the sight of more than twenty doctors, all fully outfitted by the skill of his hands, be sad? Even when Christmas was months away I'd come into his study and find him with the wooden chest out, armloads of fabric and stockings and tinsel wings spread around him. He used to do his own make-up too, practising different 'looks' well in advance of the big day. In all my life I have never known a person possess more cosmetics and lotions than he; he almost had too many bottles, jars, creams.

Still, these kinds of thoughts did not flourish then; these were the fine days of my mother's talent. Her studio seemed always filled with light and the pleasant sound of her humming as she worked. Moma wore a yellow smock for painting, we were all three of us in costume of one sort or another. Blotched bright all over her front were the colours she used: vermilion, emerald, clear sea blue. They formed a pattern there, like she herself was a pretty canvas. Her cheeks too might be smudged with paint; she would have stepped back from her work to consider it, resting her face in her hands, thinking. I knew that gesture well. She was so calm and lovely then. When she took her hands away, colour was there.

How different that unknown mark upon her from the painstaking detail that went into my father's Christmas face. First he creamed his whole face in, smoothing the shadows away from under his eyes and carrying the pale colour all the way down from temple to jawline. Only when his features were blank and perfect as one of my mother's canvases did he begin the detailed work: drawing in the fine line of black that outlined his eyes, painting over the lids a film of shimmering blue. He filled his pale eyebrows in until they were dark and exciting-looking and after he had coloured his lips a juicy red he used Vaseline to make them shiny and wet. 'Cherry ripe' he used to say.

By contrast, Moma in her studio worked earnestly in flat colours. With a broad knife she scooped up the thick oil from her palette and spread it like softened butter across the canvas, working the pigment in with the palm of her hand until the whole surface was deeply stained. The clean scent of her work rose from the floor where she was crouched over it, painting the last quick lines that were her signature. Without looking up she'd say 'Hi' when I came in. 'Had a good day at school? Miss me while you there?'

These things, as I remember them, seem like nice times for a girl. Even my Dad working late most nights didn't disturb the impression we three were happy together. Moma and I ate our supper at the big table in the dining room, waiting, listening, like a TV family, for the sound of his car in the driveway. Then, when he walked in the door we both ran up and kissed him and he put his arms around us and called us 'my girls'.

'What have my two girls been doing today?'

'How's my big girl?'

'How's my little girl?'

As he sat at the table, eating the meal Moma had kept warm for him in the hostess tray, I watched my parents together. My mother, changed into a new dress for the evening, the scent of linseed warm like fragrance on her skin and my Dad sometimes reaching out to take her hand, to stroke it. How I loved it when he did that to Moma, and how she seemed to need it too. She put her own hand over his, then leaned over and kissed him with her mouth.

Cherry ripe.

*

All wives were behaving that way towards husbands in the early sixties. That was what my mother said, much later, when everything had changed.

'We were putting up, honey. We were dealing, but that's all we were doing. I was an innocent when you were young. I had no idea your father was the way he was. No one will understand this now but when I married him I really believed he would be a husband. All the fairy days were nothing to me, I believed, I believed . . .'

I was grown up by then but still I put my hands to my ears and ran from the room like a little girl. I too had glimpsed my father beneath his white doctor's coat, knew how manly his dark suit had been.

'All the time he was lying to me,' my mother, in the next room, talked on. I put a pillow over my head but even then could hear the sound of her, talking to herself maybe but the words coming out to find rest in me. 'I never knew . . . I never guessed. Now my life is over and I feel like such a fool . . .'

From now on, I guess she'll always be that kind of woman. Yet there was a time when she had a family, a career, and a turkey to slice when my Dad's fairy parade was done. It took me to change all that, the quiet daughter you should never trust. We could have had Christmas Days the same forever had it not been for that one day, the last, had it not been for me.

I was ten years old. I remember because the parade dresses were based on Swan Lake which my dad had taken me to see earlier in the year for a birthday treat. When we came out of the dark matinée theatre into the brightness of the afternoon, his eyes were shining.

'That's it, Francie! This year I'll do white tulle and swansdown. I'll make the dresses ankle length and petticoat them so they come out to here . . .' He swept his arms around him in a circle. 'What do you think?'

In the months that followed he worked hard on the idea, in the evenings drawing up patterns for different designs, then experimenting with cloth, cut, and sewing right up to the weekend before

Christmas Day when suddenly the dresses were nearly done and he was stitching white beads on to the bodices, a thick crust of them like frost, and all by hand. Although when they were finished they were to me not as beautiful on the bulky forms of the doctors as they had been on the ballerinas in the theatre, still my Dad was so slim in his gown he was dainty. He'd put on a special cream that looked plain white in the jar until he dipped his fingers in and they came out sparkling with a million trillion glittery bits. Gently, he applied these to his cheekbones, his throat, his shoulders, patting the cream down so the tiny stars became affixed. When he took up his wand, and turned, twinkling in the light, my heart stopped. If a real fairy had asked me what I wanted most in the world, I would have wished for a pot of that glitter. More than any of my Dad's outfits or silver shoes, I wanted my fingers deep in the jar, to bring them out rich with stars.

Christmas that year we had a guest in the house. He was a colleague, my Dad said, 'on loan'. He came all the way from another hospital up north and it was my Dad's job to show him around Victoria Grand, teach him about hearts. He was a tall man, I remember, and completely bald, the skin stretched tight over his forehead so his whole head was taut and shiny as a sheath.

'Your dad looks great, doesn't he?'

I was watching the parade with him in the hospital. I was even holding his hand. Across the ward, my Dad was running around the beds with the other doctors just like they did every year.

'Twinkle, twinkle!' they called out to the sick and dying.

'Happy Christmas to you!'

As usual, it seemed everyone was laughing; even if they couldn't sit up in bed properly, patients loved my Dad's Christmas show.

'I'll make your wish come true!' one fairy doctor said to an old lady lying on her back. 'I'm your little bit of Christmas magic . . .' He pirouetted for her and though she couldn't move her head at all, I saw that she was smiling. 'Happy Christmas to you . . .'

In the midst of all the swan dresses and the dancing I saw my Dad looking around, looking for me, I thought, at first, but it was the man whose hand I held he was seeking. When he found him, their eyes met. He smiled. For seconds, it seemed a lifetime to me, they were held together in stillness amidst all the bright whirl of the room, the swirl of white organza skirts, the laughter. Then my Dad came running over to us and tapped us both upon the shoulder with his tinsel wand. That was all he did. Yet, though I was left bare of his touch, a fragment of the wand's silver stayed on the man's jacket, glittering. Then I knew. Knew enough to watch them for the rest of the morning, watch them when we went home to my mother's turkey meal, watch them in the bathroom together, my father pretending to take his make-up off, the other following. Through the crack of the door I saw them with each other, the expert speed of their hands, placement of kisses, my Dad's wet mouth.

Cherry ripe.

I'm the guilty one who told my Moma all.

Today, I don't call her Moma. I use her real name, Marjorie, when we talk on the telephone. She tells me about her job in the art supplies shop, the people she meets. Her own painting she gave up on years ago. I'm not sure that she writes letters to Clement Greenberg or any of those people any more. Even so, she seems pleased enough with her life.

'Contented,' she says.

She still wants to talk about her marriage years with me but even now I can't hear any of it.

'You should get in touch with your father,' she tells me. 'You know, he and I have found friendship over the years, I'm sure you could too . . .'

After my Dad left home I couldn't talk to anyone for a long time. Now I understand why he so loved the theatre, the costumes and disguise . . . but it took me a while to discover that. The more layers you can put on to yourself the safer you become, and quieter. Years later, and, like him, I've become a doctor, I specialize in hearts. When I started out in medical school I couldn't so much as dissect a soft mouse or round sheep's eye, but now that I'm fully adult, in my own dark suits, white coat, I can cut and cut. Although I have many friends, play golf, and go out on dinner dates most weekends, I am actually a very lonely person: unlike my Dad, I lack the real ability to transform. When he sent for his clothes, he left behind all the dresses he'd made, the trunk full of petal skirts and wings, the tinsel trims, even the little pot of glittery cream he left for me to play with.

'Let Francie be the Christmas fairy from now on,' his letter said.

But I threw all the lovely things away.

home for christmas

anne macleod

'I'm sorry, Madam, there's no sign of your reservation here.' The bored girl in Departures peered over the computer screen.

'But I've had this ticket for months!' Catherine exploded. 'And it's been so hard getting to Heathrow today! You've probably filled my seat with a standby passenger. But I'm only two minutes late, so you can just unfill it. You'll get me to Inverness tonight, one way or another!'

The girl sighed. 'Will you let me have your ticket? I'll try running it through again . . . it might be computer error.'

She pecked at the keyboard and waited expectantly. She pecked again. No obvious response. Catherine looked round at the queue. It was getting longer, but still good-natured. It was Christmas, after all.

'There you are, Madam, that seems to be in order now. We apologize for any inconvenience caused. Have you luggage for the hold?'

'Yes, but I'll take this with me,' said Catherine, heaving her suitcase on to the counter, and keeping back the canvas bag that held her Christmas presents.

The attendant flickered surprise at the state of the suitcase, but she stowed it without comment in a plastic crate and handed Catherine a boarding pass.

'Gate 41. Fifteen minutes.'

'I can see you're wondering . . .' began Catherine nervously. 'I was nearly caught in the Regent Street explosion this afternoon. Luckily my case took the worst of it . . .'

But the girl had already turned to the next passenger, and the words bounced off her unresponsive back. Catherine picked up her bag and walked twice around the terminal before she found Gate 41.

As she limped along, she wished that she'd waited to have her leg examined. It should have been X-rayed, really. But they took so long in Casualty, and she didn't want to miss her flight. She'd booked the seat in October. She knew how busy they were on Christmas Eve.

It was four o'clock, but the shops and stalls bulged with people, smiling, noisy, excited. If Catherine hadn't felt dizzy, and been so short of time, she'd have liked to wander through them all, they were so bright, so alive. She'd have spent a lot of money too, not that she needed more presents. Not that she'd any money left in her bank account. Well, that wasn't strictly true. Her pay should be in by now.

The papers at the bookstall caught her eye.

FOUR KILLED IN CITY OUTRAGE, the headlines clamoured. KILLERS AT CHRISTMAS. TERROR ATTACK ON XMAS EVE.

She'd been lucky to get through town at all.

The young nurse in Casualty had smiled as she took her name, and asked about the shoulder bag she clutched so tightly.

'Christmas presents,' Catherine whispered. 'For my folk in Inverness. I've a little niece and nephew there. I'm flying up this evening.'

Her eyes filled with tears. She felt weak. It was the shock.

'I'll be back in two ticks,' the girl promised, but she wouldn't be. Catherine could see they were rushed, could read the unspoken apology. And she had to catch the plane. So she took herself off to the ladies, and washed all her cuts as best she could with the hospital soap and paper towels. She bound the deep gash in her thigh with torn strips of petticoat. Just like the ancient westerns, except that her petticoat wasn't flannel. Polyester cotton. It didn't work very well. She had to pad it with paper tissues.

Her coat was luckily quite unmarked and hid the damage to her skirt.

Thank goodness, she thought, for the British Warm.

The trench-coat covered everything.

She made good her escape, winking at the porter who held the door. Her luck held. Though the underground was congested, she managed to get a seat nearly all the way. It's a long ride from central London to Heathrow. She should have stopped for coffee, but she hadn't enough time. They'd feed her on the plane anyway.

She thought about buying a paper, but decided against it. She'd catch the news later, once she was home and more relaxed. Not that it was strictly her home. Since her brother's marriage she'd spent every Christmas with him and his wife. She and Allan had always been close, with losing their parents so young. No, she shook her head, they'd always been close. The accident brought them closer.

Catherine arrived at Gate 41, with a minimum of fuss. That was surprising. There was usually more of a song and dance in Security. But then, she thought, with the bomb they're probably targeting flights abroad, and Ireland, that's only natural. She collapsed in a torn bucket chair, grateful for its rigidity. She was shattered. She could sleep on the plane, but she must keep awake till then. Her leg hurt. That helped. She concentrated on the pain.

The pain grew worse as she limped towards the aircraft, and she boarded the plane in acute discomfort. The stewardess smiled and nodded, and Catherine relaxed at last, as the flight slipped into its old familiar pattern. Safety drill, drinks . . . she didn't order. By then, she was asleep.

They arrived in Inverness, almost as soon as they left Heathrow, or so it seemed. Catherine felt better except for her leg. It was sore and stiff and slightly numb. She wasn't quite sure where her foot was.

As she crossed the tarmac at Dalcross, the feeling returned with a vengeance. This was welcome, despite the pain, for she had to drive home. Her brother had left his car keys at the main desk for her, their usual arrangement.

For ages, she hung around the desk, waiting for someone to help her. The gift shop was still busy, and the check-in desk was mobbed. Nobody seemed responsible for reception. No one took any notice of Catherine standing there. She waited with growing impatience, feeling weaker all the time.

Finally, uncomfortable and cross, she reached over the high desk and lifted the keys which lay there; left rather carelessly, she thought, in plain view. She knew these were her brother's keys, she recognized the key ring. She'd bought it on a holiday in Spain that summer. She wanted to lodge a formal complaint about the lack of service, but there was no one to receive it, so she left. Office parties had a lot to answer for.

The short drive to Inverness was always difficult for her, and worse than usual in the unexpected snow. It was somewhere along this road that her parents had been killed. Catherine didn't know where, she'd been eight at the time, and if she had been told, she'd forgotten, or suppressed it. She remembered the car, a Morris Oxford, very grand. It was an ex-police car, black when they bought it. They were all very proud of it. Their father resprayed it – white, which Catherine adored. She loved the car, the colour, the leather seats. The comfort. It was the most intense of all her childhood pleasures.

They said it was nobody's fault, the accident. A lorry went out of control on the twisting road and that was it. How do you cope with a loss like that? Catherine wasn't sure. They'd stayed with successive relatives, she and Allan. She left school at seventeen, trained as a teacher, and lived and worked in London after that. She had a flat, but it wasn't home. She was still single.

When Allan married and set up home in Inverness, she'd come back to visit, very much on the defensive. But the town had changed beyond all recognition, and Allan was so happy in his marriage, and Sophie, his bride, so welcoming . . . Catherine's reservations fled like frost in a spring garden. The ghosts were laid to rest.

They'd had a son first, and now a baby daughter for Catherine to love and lavish attention on. She hadn't seen the baby, who was to be christened on Christmas Day – Sophia Catherine, with Catherine as godmother. She was Johnnie's godmother too, and they were very good friends. At four, he knew and loved his Auntie Kate, despite all the distances between them.

On her way in from the airport, Catherine drove past Stuart

Castle, a turreted house she and Allan had always thought was haunted. They used to be frightened to pass it, even in daylight. Now light shone from windows which before had been boarded up. There were no more ghosts, the only wraiths the snowflakes that swirled about the car, now thick, now thin, seductive. Rounding the corner towards the railway bridge she glanced in her mirror and saw a white car following; caught like her in the timeless, mesmerizing snow.

She switched on the radio just in time to catch a local carol service. It helped her concentration. The leg still hurt. It had started bleeding again, and she could feel the warm blood seeping through her makeshift bandage. But she was nearly home.

Allan lived on the outskirts of Inverness, and Catherine reached the house quite quickly. She drew up to the gates, which were always kept shut, and leaving the headlights on and engine running, she slipped out to open them. It was dark now, and the snow had stopped. The lights of Inverness wavered in the distance. She could see as far as the Leachkin, and over to North Kessock; the town opened to her like a dying rose, bigger, always bigger than she remembered. It was cold and the sky had cleared. The young moon lay on its back. The frost would be sharp on the covering snow.

She could feel blood trickling down her leg; she was weak and tired, and the gates were stiff and heavy. She brushed the snow off them, and managed to open one, but the other stuck fast. She couldn't budge it, try as she might. Reaching into the car for the precious shoulder bag, she crept quietly up the drive.

The house was transfigured with light and warmth, no curtain shut against the night. Catherine paused at the living-room window, rested her bag on the sill. She saw her brother and nephew hard at work. They were carefully decorating a tall Christmas tree, Allan placing the ornaments as Johnnie retrieved them. He almost fell in the huge box each time he reached into it. A real tree this year, Catherine noted.

She watched for some minutes, unnoticed and lonely. She envied her brother his family. No, that was wrong; she was part of it. The warmth extended even to her solitude in Epsom.

The electronic bleat of Allan's phone intervened. It grew louder and louder, ever more insistent. Sophie called, 'Allan, Allan . . . will you get that? I'm busy with the baby.'

As Allan disappeared, Johnnie glanced up at the window. In his hand he held an angel, whose stiff baroque robes flew upwards to eternity. He smiled and waved.

'Auntie Kate!' he cried, excited, as his father returned to the room, phone in hand. Allan was pale. He shook his head in disbelief.

'No,' he said. 'That can't be right. I'll get you my wife. This makes no sense.'

'Sophie!' he called hoarsely. 'Sophie! Come and take this call. It's the London police . . . but they're wrong, tell them they're wrong. They can't be right . . .'

'Auntie Kate!' Johnnie ran to the window.

Catherine turned at the sound of a horn. Below her in the road, a white car purred smoothly, waiting. She hadn't blocked the road, surely? She'd thought she was far enough over the pavement to leave the way free. As she watched, a female figure emerged from the passenger door; she waved and called, 'Catherine! Catherine!'

The voice was dear and familiar as her own breathing, and Catherine, leaving her shoulder bag propped on the window-sill, moved slowly down the path towards the waiting Oxford, uncertainty disappearing with each painful step.

'What's wrong, Allan?' Sophie knelt by his side.

'Tell them they're wrong. It can't be Catherine. Tell them they're wrong. They must be wrong.'

Sophie took the phone from his shaking hand, and cradling the baby in one arm, spoke uncertainly, 'Hello? What's going on? Can I help at all?'

Allan hunched his shoulders, staring blankly at the open fire, but Johnnie ran to his side. 'Auntie Kate!' he insisted. He pointed to the window. Allan followed blindly, then stopped. There were lights in the drive, a bag on the window-sill.

'Catherine!'

He rushed to the door and out into the waiting night, its silence churned by the Metro's idling. Even as he listened, the engine stuttered and died.

In the light that spilled from the house, he saw a dark thin trail stretching in crisp new snow from the window to the driveway. He knelt and scooped a handful of that darker snow. In stronger light, it bloomed red, was strangely viscous. It stained his fingers.

And in the harsh headlights he could see, too well, that there were no footprints but his own.

the junky's christmas

william s. burroughs

It was Christmas Day and Danny the Car Wiper hit the street junk-sick and broke after seventy-two hours in the precinct jail. It was a clear bright day, but there was no warmth in the sun. Danny shivered with an inner cold. He turned up the collar of his worn, greasy black overcoat.

This beat benny wouldn't pawn for a deuce, he thought.

He was in the West Nineties. A long block of brownstone rooming houses. Here and there a holy wreath in a clean black window. Danny's senses registered everything sharp and clear, with the painful intensity of junk sickness. The light hurt his dilated eyes.

He walked past a car, darting his pale blue eyes sideways in quick appraisal. There was a package on the seat and one of the ventilator windows was unlocked. Danny walked on ten feet. No one in sight. He snapped his fingers and went through a pantomime of remembering something, and wheeled around. No one.

A bad setup, he decided. *The street being empty like this, I stand out conspicuous. Gotta make it fast.*

He reached for the ventilator window. A door opened behind him. Danny whipped out a rag and began polishing the car windows. He could feel the man standing behind him.

'What're yuh doin'?'

Danny turned as if surprised. 'Just thought your car windows needed polishing, mister.'

The man had a frog face and a Deep South accent. He was wearing a camel's-hair overcoat.

'My caah don't need polishin' or nothing stole out of it neither.'

Danny slid sideways as the man grabbed for him. 'I wasn't lookin' to steal nothing, mister. I'm from the South too. Florida –'

'Goddamned sneakin' thief!'

Danny walked away fast and turned a corner.

Better get out of the neighborhood. That hick is likely to call the law.

He walked fifteen blocks. Sweat ran down his body. There was a raw ache in his lungs. His lips drew back off his yellow teeth in a snarl of desperation.

I gotta score somehow. If I had some decent clothes . . .

Danny saw a suitcase standing in a doorway. Good leather. He stopped and pretended to look for a cigarette.

Funny, he thought. *No one around. Inside maybe, phoning for a cab.*

The corner was only a few houses away. Danny took a deep breath and picked up the suitcase. He made the corner. Another block, another corner. The case was heavy.

I got a score here all right, he thought. *Maybe enough for a sixteenth and a room.* Danny shivered and twitched, feeling a warm room and heroin emptying into his vein. *Let's have a quick look.*

He stepped into Morningside Park. No one around.

Jesus, I never see the town this empty.

He opened the suitcase. Two long packages in brown wrapping paper. He took one out. It felt like meat. He tore the package open at one end, revealing a woman's naked foot. The toenails were painted with purple-red polish. He dropped the leg with a sneer of disgust.

'Holy Jesus!' he exclaimed. 'The routines people put down these days. Legs! Well, I got a case anyway.' He dumped the other leg out. No bloodstains. He snapped the case shut and walked away.

'Legs!' he muttered.

He found the Buyer sitting at a table in Jarrow's Cafeteria.

'Thought you might be taking the day off,' Danny said, putting the case down.

The Buyer shook his head sadly. 'I got nobody. So what's Christmas to me?' His eyes traveled over the case, poking, testing, looking for flaws. 'What was in it?'

'Nothing.'

'What's the matter? I don't pay enough?'

'I tell you there wasn't nothing in it.'

'Okay. So somebody travels with an empty suitcase. Okay.' He held up three fingers.

'For Christ's sake, Gimpy, give me a nickel.'

'You got somebody else. Why don't he give you a nickel?'

'It's like I say, the case was empty.'

Gimpy kicked at the case disparagingly. 'It's all nicked up and kinda dirty-looking.' He sniffed suspiciously. 'How come it stink like that? Mexican leather?'

'So am I in the leather business?'

Gimpy shrugged. 'Could be.' He pulled out a roll of bills and peeled off three ones, dropping them on the table behind the napkin dispenser. 'You want?'

'Okay.' Danny picked up the money. 'You see George the Greek?' he asked.

'Where you been? He got busted two days ago.'

'Oh . . . That's bad.'

Danny walked out. *Now where can I score?* he thought. George the Greek had lasted so long, Danny thought of him as permanent. *It was good H too, and no short counts.*

Danny went up to 103rd and Broadway. Nobody in Jarrow's. Nobody in the Automat.

'Yeah,' he snarled. 'All the pushers off on the nod someplace. What they care about anybody else? So long as they get it in the vein. What they care about a sick junky?'

He wiped his nose with one finger, looking around furtively.

No use hitting those jigs in Harlem. Like as not get beat for my money or they slip me rat poison. Might find Pantopon Rose at Eighth and 23rd.

There was no one he knew in the 23rd Street Thompson's.

Jesus, he thought. *Where is everybody?*

He clutched his coat collar together with one hand, looking up and down the street. *There's Joey from Brooklyn. I'd know that hat anywhere.*

'Joey. Hey, Joey!'

Joey was walking away, with his back to Danny. He turned around. His face was sunken, skull-like. The grey eyes glittered under a greasy grey felt hat. Joey was sniffing at regular intervals and his eyes were watering.

No use asking him, Danny thought. They looked at each other with the hatred of disappointment.

'Guess you heard about George the Greek,' Danny said.

'Yeah. I heard. You been up to 103rd?'

'Yeah. Just came from there. Nobody around.'

'Nobody around anyplace,' Joey said. 'I can't even score for goof-balls.'

'Well, Merry Christmas, Joey. See you.'

'Yeah. See you.'

Danny was walking fast. He had remembered a croaker on 18th Street. Of course the croaker had told him not to come back. Still, it was worth trying.

A brownstone house wtih a card in the window: *P.H.Zunniga, M.D.* Danny rang the bell. He heard slow steps. The door opened, and the doctor looked at Danny with bloodshot brown eyes. He was weaving slightly and supported his plump body against the door-jamb. His face was smooth, Latin, the little red mouth slack. He said nothing. He just leaned there, looking at Danny.

Goddamned alcoholic, Danny thought. He smiled.

'Merry Christmas, Doctor.'

The doctor did not reply.

'You remember me, Doctor.' Danny tried to edge past the doctor, into the house. 'I'm sorry to trouble you on Christmas Day, but I've suffered another attack.'

'Attack?'

'Yes. Facial neuralgia.' Danny twisted one side of his face into a horrible grimace. The doctor recoiled slightly, and Danny pushed into the dark hallway.

'Better shut the door or you'll be catching cold,' he said jovially, shoving the door shut.

The doctor looked at him, his eyes focusing visibly. 'I can't give you a prescription,' he said.

'But Doctor, this is a legitimate condition. An emergency, you understand.'

'No prescription. Impossible. It's against the law.'

'You took an oath, Doctor. I'm in agony.' Danny's voice shot up to a hysterical grating whine.

The doctor winced and passed a hand over his forehead.

'Let me think. I can give you one quarter-grain tablet. That's all I have in the house.'

'But, Doctor – a quarter G . . .'

The doctor stopped him. 'If your condition is legitimate, you will not need more. If it isn't, I don't want anything to do with you. Wait right here.'

The doctor weaved down the hall, leaving a wake of alcoholic breath. He came back and dropped a tablet into Danny's hand. Danny wrapped the tablet in a piece of paper and tucked it away.

'There is no charge.' The doctor put his hand on the doorknob. 'And now, my dear . . .'

'But, Doctor – can't you inject the medication?'

'No. You will obtain longer relief in using orally. Please not to return.' The doctor opened the door.

Well, this will take the edge off, and I still have money to put down on a room, Danny thought.

He knew a drugstore that sold needles without question. He bought a 26-gauge insulin needle and an eyedropper, which he selected carefully, rejecting models with a curved dropper or a thick end. Finally he bought a baby pacifier, to use instead of the bulb. He stopped in the Automat and stole a teaspoon.

Danny put down two dollars on a six-dollar-a-week room in the West Forties, where he knew the landlord. He bolted the door and put his spoon, needle and dropper on a table by the bed. He dropped the tablet in the spoon and covered it with a dropperful of water. He held a match under the spoon until the tablet dissolved. He tore a strip of paper, wet it and wrapped it around the end of the dropper, fitting the needle over the wet paper to make an airtight connection. He dropped a piece of lint from his pocket into the spoon and sucked the liquid into the dropper through the needle, holding the needle in the lint to take up the last drop.

Danny's hands trembled with excitement and his breath was quick. With a shot in front of him, his defenses gave way, and junk sickness flooded his body. His legs began to twitch and ache. A cramp stirred in his stomach. Tears ran down his face from his smarting, burning eyes. He wrapped a handkerchief around his right arm, holding the end in his teeth. He tucked the handkerchief in, and began rubbing his arm to bring out a vein.

Guess I can hit that one, he thought, running one finger along a vein. He picked up the dropper in his left hand.

Danny heard a groan from the next room. He frowned with annoyance. Another groan. He could not help listening. He walked across the room, the dropper in his hand, and inclined his ear to the wall. The groans were coming at regular intervals, a horrible inhuman sound pushed out from the stomach.

Danny listened for a full minute. He returned to the bed and sat down. *Why don't someone call a doctor?* he thought indignantly. *It's a bringdown*. He straightened his arm and poised the needle. He tilted his head, listening again.

Oh, for Christ's sake! He tore off the handkerchief and placed the dropper in a water glass, which he hid behind the wastebasket. He stepped into the hall and knocked on the door of the next room. There was no answer. The groans continued. Danny tried the door. It was open.

The shade was up and the room was full of light. He had expected an old person somehow, but the man on the bed was very young, eighteen or twenty, fully clothed and doubled up, with his hands clasped across his stomach.

'What's wrong, kid?' Danny asked.

The boy looked at him, his eyes blank with pain. Finally he got out one word: 'Kidneys.'

'Kidney stones?' Danny smiled. 'I don't mean it's funny, kid. It's just . . . I've faked it so many times. Never saw the real thing before. I'll call an ambulance.'

The boy bit his lip. 'Won't come. Doctors won't come.' The boy hid his face in the pillow.

Danny nodded. 'They figure it's just another junky throwing a wingding for a shot. But your case is legit. Maybe if I went to the hospital and explained things . . . No, I guess that wouldn't be so good.'

'Don't live here,' the boy said, his voice muffled. 'They say I'm not entitled.'

'Yeah, I know how they are, the bureaucrat bastards. I had a friend once, died of snakebite right in the waiting room. They wouldn't even listen when he tried to explain a snake bit him. He never had enough moxie. That was fifteen years ago, down in Jacksonville. . . .'

Danny trailed off. Suddenly he put out his thin, dirty hand and touched the boy's shoulder.

'I – I'm sorry, kid. You wait. I'll fix you up.'

He went back to his room and got the dropper, and returned to the boy's room.

'Roll up your sleeve, kid.' The boy fumbled his coat sleeve with a weak hand.

'That's okay. I'll get it.' Danny undid the shirt button at the wrist and pushed the shirt and coat up, baring a thin brown forearm. Danny hesitated, looking at the dropper. Sweat ran down his nose. The boy was looking up at him. Danny shoved the needle in the boy's forearm and watched the liquid drain into the flesh. He straightened up.

The boy's face began to relax. He sat up and smiled.

'Say, that stuff really works,' he said. 'You a doctor, mister?'

'No, kid.'

The boy lay down, stretching. 'I feel real sleepy. Didn't sleep all last night.' His eyes were closing.

Danny walked across the room and pulled the shade down. He went back to his room and closed the door without locking it. He sat on the bed, looking at the empty dropper. It was getting dark outside. Danny's body ached for junk, but it was a dull ache now, dull and hopeless. Numbly, he took the needle off the dropper and wrapped it in a piece of paper. Then he wrapped the needle and dropper together. He sat there with the package in his hand. *Gotta stash this someplace*, he thought.

Suddenly a warm flood pulsed through his veins and broke in his head like a thousand golden speedballs.

For Christ's sake, Danny thought. *I must have scored for the immaculate fix!*

The vegetable serenity of junk settled in his tissues. His face went slack and peaceful, and his head fell forward.

Danny the Car Wiper was on the nod.

biographical notes

The editor
Elisa Segrave writes short stories and articles and is currently writing a book on illness.

The contributors
Mary Broke Freeman trained as a fashion journalist in the sixties in Paris on *Queen* magazine and *Jardin des Modes*. While housebound with babies she began writing fiction and has had stories for both adults and children published and broadcast. Her novel *Return to a Dream* was published in 1994.

William S. Burroughs is the author of the classics *Junky* and *The Naked Lunch* as well as many other works. He is a member of the American Academy of Arts and Letters. He divides his time between New York City and Lawrence, Kansas.

Miriam Frank is of German-Jewish and Lithuanian-American origin. She grew up in Spain, France, Mexico and New Zealand before settling in London where she studied medicine, married a painter, raised two daughters and became a senior lecturer and consultant in a teaching hospital.

Kirsty Gunn's stories have appeared in *First Fictions: Introduction 11*, *Slow Dancer* magazine and the Serpent's Tail anthology *Border Lines*. Her first novel, *Rain*, was published in 1994. She lives in London.

Michele Hanson is a freelance journalist and short story writer. Her book *Treasure, the Trials of a Teenage Terror*, based on her weekly columns in the *Guardian*, was published in 1993.

Tim Hutchinson is a young writer, artist and illustrator. He is at present writing short stories and writing and illustrating a book for children.

Kelvin Christopher James was born in Trinidad. His stories have appeared in US magazines – *Bomb, Between C & D* and *American Letters and Commentary*. In 1992 he published *Jumping Ship and other stories* and in 1993 *Secrets*, a novel about a teenage girl on a Caribbean island. He lives in Harlem.

Sheena Joughin is writing a book of stories about living in west London with her five-year-old son, and having holidays in Yorkshire. She is of Irish origin.

A.L. Kennedy was born in Dundee in 1965. She was chosen as one of Granta's Best of Young British Novelists for her novel *Looking for the Possible Dance*. She has published two collections of stories – *Night Geometry and the Garscadden Trains* and *Now that You're Back* – and *The Audition*, a drama.

Francis King was born in Switzerland in 1923 and spent his childhood in India. His years in the British Council took him to Italy, Greece, Egypt, Finland and Japan. In 1963 he resigned to devote himself entirely to writing. In 1993 he published his autobiography *Yesterday Came Suddenly*.

Mark Kurlansky is an American writer, the author of *A Continent of Islands; Searching for a Caribbean Destiny* and *A Chosen Few: the Resurrection of European Jewry*. He frequently writes about the Caribbean which he covered for seven years as a journalist.

Mandla Langa was born in 1950 and educated in South Africa. He was forced into exile in 1976. He has published poetry, short stories and two novels – *Rainbow on the Paper Sky* and *Tenderness of Blood*.

Anne Macleod was born in Scotland of Anglo–Irish parents. She studied medicine at the University of Aberdeen and now lives and works in the Highlands. She has published poetry and prose in various anthologies.

Seán Mac Mathúna lives in Dublin where he works as a scriptwriter for television. He has had two anthologies of short stories published. He has also written a collection for children. Two years ago his play *The Winter Thief* was produced by the Abbey Theatre, Dublin.

Andrew O'Hagan was born in Glasgow in 1968 and grew up with seagulls and submarines on the Ayrshire coast. An assistant editor of *The London Review of Books*, he has written articles and appeared on television in Britain and the USA.

Omar Sattaur was born in Georgetown, Guyana, and educated in Britain. He is a freelance journalist living in Kathmandu. This is his first published fiction.

William Trevor was born in Cork in 1928 and educated at Trinity College Dublin. In 1964 he won the Hawthornden Prize for his book *The Old Boys* and in 1991 he was runner-up for the Booker Prize for his novel *Reading Turgenev*. His collection of essays *Excursions into the Real World* and his latest book *Felicia's Journey* came out in 1994.

Frank Tuohy's novel *The Ice Saints* won the James Tait Black Memorial Prize and the Geoffrey Faber Memorial Award. His collection of stories *The Admiral and the Nuns* won the first Katherine Mansfield Short Story Prize.

Founded in 1986, Serpent's Tail publishes the innovative and the challenging.

If you would like to receive a catalogue of our current publications please write to:

FREEPOST
Serpent's Tail
4 Blackstock Mews
LONDON N4 2BR

(No stamp necessary if your letter is posted in the United Kingdom.)